# Fred Boggitt and the Loch Ness Monster

by

Jenny Tuxford & Jenny Brazier

authorHOUSE®

*AuthorHouse™ UK Ltd.*
*500 Avebury Boulevard*
*Central Milton Keynes, MK9 2BE*
*www.authorhouse.co.uk*
*Phone: 08001974150*

*First published by AuthorHouse 1/4/2010*

*ISBN: 978-1-4389-9593-9 (sc)*

*This book is printed on acid-free paper.*

*The Clansman Hotel is a real hotel. I borrowed the name. But the name is the only part that is real. Everything else relating to the hotel, in this book, is entirely fictional.*

To our dear families and friends, to Brownies and Guides everywhere and pupils, past and present.

# Chapter 1

It was the Easter holidays. The Boggitt family were off to spend a week camping at the 'Bit of Peace and Quiet Caravan and Campsite' on the shores of Loch Ness. Spirits were high as they began their expedition, very early, one chilly morning.

Mr. Boggitt had already treated his family to several verses of 'The Wee Cooper of Fife' and 'Ye Canna Shove Your Granny off a Bus', before the satellite navigation system eventually detected their position on the Slough bypass and directed them onwards to the M40 motorway.

"This is the life, eh Mother?" Mr. Boggitt called over his shoulder. "There's nothing like this feeling is there? Just knowing that you've got a whole week of peace and tranquillity, away from the hustle and bustle of town."

"This isn't the quickest way to the M40 you know," Granny shouted, sucking noisily on her sherbet lemon. "I don't know why you bother with that starlight navigation thingy. I could've shown you a much better way."

Granny was sitting squashed up in the back with Fred and Mrs. Boggitt. Mr. Boggitt was driving, of course, while Fred's dog, Monty, was occupying the front passenger seat and was busily sniffing the upholstery and scratching himself.

"Father's doing all right by my reckoning," Mrs. Boggitt said, stopping her knitting for an instant while she peered at the map book over the top of her glasses.

"Shouldn't you have the book the other way round mum?" Fred muttered. "Only Britain looks kind of funny with Scotland at the bottom."

"You read your book Fred," his mother replied sharply, "and leave the navigating to me. I've only got the map here in case that thing (pointing to the sat. nav.) decides to take us to Scotland by way of Japan."

"And you just relax, Granny, and suck your sweets," Mr. Boggitt called, fiddling with the car heating controls.

"I wouldn't need to suck 'em if you'd let *me* sit in the front seat instead of that blessed dog."

"Now, now! You know he gets car sick, don't you old chum?" Mr. Boggitt said, taking a hand off the wheel momentarily to give the mongrel a pat.

"And so do I, as you well know! *And* I get indi....

Oh no!" Granny gasped, nearly swallowing her sherbet lemon. "I've forgotten my indigestion tablets! You'll have to go back Fred senior. I can't last a whole week without my indigestion tablets."

"*I'm not going back now and that's a fact!* I asked you *ten times* if you'd got everything!" Mr. Boggitt bellowed, his good mood suddenly evaporating like the early morning mist. "Tell her Mother!"

"Now look what you've made me go and do. I've dropped a stitch. Calm down both of you," Mrs. Boggitt said, going very red in the face. "I'll get you some tablets when we stop at a service station."

Granny's grunt was her only reply.

"I sincerely hope *you've* got everything young Fred?" Mr. Boggitt said with false cheerfulness, trying to make up for his sudden spell of bad temper.

There was no reply. Fred licked a finger and turned over the page of his little paperback, 'Spotlight on the Elusive Loch Ness Monster'.

"Dad," he said, after a little while, "what does elusive mean?"

"Well now, son," Mr. Boggitt replied, scratching his head and thinking hard. "I should think it's from a Latin word and it-um- means-um-like when you *elude* something. You've heard of the Scarlet Pimpernel haven't you? Well, he was elusive."

There was no reply from the back seat.

# Chapter 2

It was an *extremely* long journey up to Scotland, broken only by a few brief stops at Motorway cafés.

The words that every driver dreads, "Are we nearly there yet?" were uttered so many times that at last Mr. Boggitt snapped,

"Granny, if you say that one more time I'll drop you off at the next service station."

After what she regarded as a totally un-called for telling off, when she'd only been expressing an entirely natural interest in their progress up the country, Granny lapsed into total silence. She pulled her poncho tightly round her and promptly fell asleep.

So long was the trip that Mrs. Boggitt would have finished the pea-green jumper she was knitting for her husband, except for the fact that she was rapidly running out of wool.

"Do you know, this pattern's all wrong, Dad," she said, leaning forwards in her seat and prodding him with one of her knitting needles to attract his attention.

"No, I don't think so. You sing it and I'll hum along," Mr. Boggitt sniggered.

Mrs. Boggitt ignored him.

"Only I specially bought three extra balls of wool and I'm *still* running out."

"You'd better start knitting faster then Mum," Mr. Boggitt quipped.

For the first few hours of the journey, Fred had regaled them all with information gleaned from his 'Elusive Monster' book.

"There've been loads of sightings of the Loch Ness Monster, you know," he breathed excitedly. "It must be very big and scary! I bet it's got fire coming out of its nose and everything, but I won't be a bit scared when I see it. Trust me on that," he added, borrowing one of his dad's favourite sayings.

"The only monster you're likely to spot is when you look in the mirror lad. *Trust me on that,*" Mr. Boggitt said, catching his wife's eye in the rear-view mirror.

"Now Fred senior, don't go spoiling the boy's fun," Mrs. Boggitt said, smiling proudly at her son.

"This many people can't all be wrong, Dad! There are *millions* of eye-witnesses," Fred said, exaggerating slightly. He flicked through the well-worn pages of his book. He'd turned down the corners of a few for quick reference. "For instance, there's one story here written by a Donald MacDonald of somewhere called Drummer er crotchit ochtie... or something."

"Aye, *story's* about right," Mr. Boggitt interrupted. "And it's Drumnadrochit," he corrected his son, rolling the letter 'r' for extra effect.

But Fred wasn't listening. "...in the year 1893 Mr. Donald MacDonald observed a huge, terrifying monster which reared up suddenly from the middle of the loch, revealing a great green and brown head with tusks like an elephant's," Fred continued.

"Rubbish!"

"It was about 13metres long, had a neck like a giraffe's and three mighty humps. Unfortunately," he read, "even though Mr. MacDonald had his camera at the ready, he failed to get a photograph."

"I'll bet he did," Mr. Boggitt smirked.

"Leave him alone, Dad. He's not hurting anyone," Mrs. Boggitt said quietly, glancing across at Granny, being anxious not to wake her.

"I don't want the lad filling his head with all this nonsense and then having nightmares. This is supposed to be a holiday."

"In 1895 a certain salmon angler ..."

"That's a strange name – even for a Scotsman," Mr. Boggitt spluttered. "How would you like to be called Mr. Salmon Angler?"

"I think that's enough for now, Fred. You read the book nicely to yourself," Mrs. Boggitt said.

6

After that it went a bit quiet in the car. Mr. Boggitt had switched the heating up to full blast, in the sudden belief that they had chosen the coldest day of the year to begin their vacation.

Monty, comfortably curled up on the front seat, had finally stopped panting and had dozed off into dreamland, having exhaled enough doggy breath to send them all into a coma.

Having exhausted his entire reserve of all things Scottish: songs, ballads and poems, Mr. Boggitt then launched into his all-too-familiar joke routine: "There was an Englishman, a Scotsman and...," until the soft (and *not* so soft) sound of snoring alerted him to the fact that he had, for the time being, lost his audience.

# Chapter 3

At long, long last a black and white chequered flag appeared on the sat. nav.'s monitor and an electronic voice announced the Boggitts' arrival at their destination. The car bumped its way across the gravel and came to rest next to a somewhat battered and worn sign which, nevertheless, proclaimed this rather desolate looking plot of land to be, 'The Bit of Peace and Quiet Caravan and Campsite'.

Mr. Boggitt opened the car door, only to have it snatched out of his hand by a rather icy wind.

Fred and Monty hopped nimbly out of the car, only too glad to escape and be out in the open air. Fred immediately began to take stock of his surroundings. After all, he'd never been much further north than Biggleswade before. Monty began chasing round and round in circles, barking at top volume.

Mrs. Boggitt emerged very tentatively, like a large, brown moth emerging from a chrysalis – only not quite so elegantly.

"Every bit of my body is complaining," she groaned as she finally managed to stand upright. "I'm completely numb." Then, "Fred Boggitt get that mad dog on a lead at once!" she bellowed. "We don't want to be kicked off the site before we've even arrived!"

Mr. Boggitt had to stoop inside the car to lever Granny from her seat, before taking several minutes to straighten her out.

"Just don't ask me to go back to England," she gasped at last. "I'll stay here, thank you very much!"

Mr. Boggitt ignored her and began jogging up and down on the spot, before bending down ten times to touch his toes and then spreading his arms and legs to perform some extremely clumsy star jumps.

Next, he clapped his hands and rubbed them together vigorously.

"Right ... well then. Here we are," he shouted, stating the obvious. He was having to yell to make his voice heard above the racket the wind was making, as it hammered the trees and bushes. "Beautiful isn't it?"

"I can't see much sign of anyone camping, can you?" Mrs. Boggitt said, mumbling through the material of her turned-up coat collar.

"Now I suggest that you three, and Monty of course, stay here and chill," Mr. Boggitt announced, glancing to his right and noticing, for the first time, the bright blue faces of his family. "Um! You three stay here and *unwind* a bit, while I go and sign in at the office and find out where we're meant to pitch our tent. I'll find out where everything is while I'm at it. All right? I won't be long," he called over his shoulder as he began loping across the car park towards a little brick building.

"I think that's the toilets, Dad," Fred called after him.

Mrs. Boggitt quickly clambered back into the car, grateful to escape from the wind.

Fred eased his brand new, deluxe, compact 10x 1 binoculars, with camouflaged rubber coating, from their case and passed the fluorescent green cord over his head. He held them up to his eyes, experimentally. He knew there were bushes and trees and fields in front of him, but all he could see was what seemed like mile after mile of sky.

"Aw!" he whined, shaking them. "I can't see anything. These stupid glasses don't work. And they came with a compass and an alarm clock and a timer *and* a stop watch *and* a torch and everything. *And* I got a carry case to put it all in. It's no use; Mum'll have to send it all back."

"Come on Fred, give 'em half a chance. You've got to get used to things," Granny said, taking the binoculars off him and walking over to a rather high hedge where Monty was busily making a large hole.

"Be patient! First, you have to turn them the right way round so that things are *magnified* you see. Then you adjust them like so, and twizzle this little knob." She pointed the glasses at Fred's face and let out a little scream. "Aaah!" she shrieked. "First sighting of the Loch Ness Monster."

Fred laughed, but his attention had been caught by the view over the top of the hedge. He didn't need his binoculars to see a dense mass of dark green trees and beyond them the grey, glittering, choppy waters of the most enormous stretch of water.

"Spectacular!" he breathed.

# Chapter 4

Mr. Boggitt returned shortly afterwards, waving bits of paper about.

"Follow me into the field," he said importantly, leading the way along a narrow path which skirted the field and led to a wooden gate. Mrs. Boggitt, Fred and Granny slipped through the hole in the hedge. Monty was already on the other side. He had found the other campers and was busily investigating their tents. However, he came bounding over to them when he was called (for once) and began sniffing out cow pats, rather as if he were detecting land mines, only unfortunately, several seconds after Granny had stepped in them.

"Oh! That's where the other campers are," Mrs. Boggitt remarked in surprise. "I should've guessed. They're getting shelter from the hedge."

"It's acting sort of like a wind-break," Fred said knowledgeably.

"Ah - there you are!" Mr. Boggitt exclaimed as he made his way over to them, seemingly rather out of breath. "How did you get there before me? Now," he said, not waiting for a reply and pointing to the far side of the field, "I suggest we pitch our tent over there by that hedge. That way we'll be away from everyone else and the hedge will act as a sort of a wind-break. Like those striped things we use at the beach, Fred," he explained.

"But Dad, isn't the wind blowing from the other direction?" Fred remarked. "*Towards* the loch?"

Mr. Boggitt licked a finger and stuck it in the air. He frowned with concentration. "Nope!" he said emphatically. "It's blowing from entirely the opposite direction. You see, Fred, winds don't always blow in the same way. They're a bit like people: unpredictable! Why, they can change tack at the drop of a hat. And there are lots of *different* winds and we give them all names, depending on where they come from and where they're blowing to. For example: there are south-easterlies and south-westerlies, not to mention north-easterlies and worth-nesterlies."

"Worth-nesterlies sound pretty severe," Granny sniggered.

"And many more which I'll tell you all about later," he said hurriedly. "And all these folk here, who've put their tents on *this* side of the field are in for a bit of a rough time tonight, believe you me," Mr. Boggitt continued, "but don't worry; they'll soon change 'em over when they see where I'm sticking ours."

"Your father knows best, son," Mrs. Boggitt said supportively, nodding her head.

"There's always a first time I suppose," Granny muttered under her breath.

"Now, I suggest that you go and get Monty out of that lady's tent, Fred, and then you take Granny and find a nice cup of tea. Here - have a look at the site-map. The café's marked. By the time you get back, Mum and I will have put up the tent and got dinner on the go. And just you wait 'til you see it," Mr. Boggitt added, winking at his wife. "It's bright green and it's got compartments so everyone can have some privacy. And talk about roomy! *And*, you'll be pleased to know, the bumf that came with it says that is – ahem – 'weatherproof, windproof, leak proof, fireproof, bombproof *and* ...," he was really laughing by now, "completely foolproof!"

# Chapter 5

"**J**ust let me get my walking stick and a pin to hold my hat on and I'll be with you."

"Which way's east Granny?" Fred asked as soon as Granny rejoined him and they were safely out of earshot. (He didn't want a lecture on the subject of compass points from his dad, when there was exploring to be done.) "Only on this map the café's to the east of the campsite."

"Well how can we find out?" Granny asked patiently, ever willing to play a part, however small, in her grandson's education.

Fred thought for a moment. He frowned with concentration.

"We could find out where the sun is and work it out from there."

"Yes, we could dear, only there isn't any sun today, in case you hadn't noticed. So how about using your new compass?" she prompted. "Only hurry up, I'm freezing to death here."

Fred spent the next few minutes ferreting about in his carrying case, but finally he found the little gadget and held it aloft.

"Ta-ra! Right! Now the compass always points to the south our teacher says, or, er, is it the north? Anyway, the map says the café's to the east so..."

"S..s..so?" Granny stammered through chattering teeth.

"So, if we walk sideways we should get there before too long," Fred announced triumphantly.

"Blow that!" said Granny, suddenly striding out. "I suggest we follow our noses. I could do with the exercise after being cooped up in that stuffy car all day. Come on! I'll race you down. There's a path here. It might even take us to the loch. It looks as if that's the way the dog's gone anyway. I can hear it barking its head off. I hope you've brought its lead."

It was a very windy day but, although it had rained fairly recently, at least the weather was dry for the moment. The path was sticky underfoot, and very uneven, but they followed it at a slow pace as it twisted its way downwards.

"Be careful," Fred cautioned as Granny skidded in her open toed sandals for the umpteenth time, looking rather like a downhill skier. "Do you want to take my hand?"

"The path's too narrow, thank you," she panted as she came to an abrupt stop and began attacking the overhanging vegetation with her walking stick. "I don't suppose there've been many people using this track yet this year. It's too early in the season."

Fred looked at his feet. His trainers were *very* muddy. He could see little doggy paw prints in the sludge where Monty had passed a little while ago – at least he supposed they belonged to Monty. He wasn't exactly known for sticking to public paths.

The trees on either side of them made a dark, shadowy tunnel, but every so often, where there was a gap, the two explorers caught a glimpse of the loch, getting nearer by the minute as the path unwound.

The clouds were low, dull and lumpy; rolling across the sky like great lumbering dinosaurs, and the water of the loch was the colour of charcoal, with little white crests topping the waves. Only one or two pleasure boats bobbed up and down on the wrinkled surface.

Then, as they rounded what turned out to be the final bend, they found themselves standing very close to the loch itself! Now there were different marks in a muddy path which seemed to follow the perimeter of the loch. It looked as if one or two bicycles had used this route, which wasn't surprising. Fred's dad had suggested that they hire some bicycles one day.

Fred breathed in deeply. "This is spectacular," he said, "absolutely spectacular! And it's huge isn't it? I didn't think it would be anything like as big as this."

"It's twenty-three miles long and a mile wide – and don't look at me like that young Fred. You're not the only one that can read a book you know!"

"I can't wait to go on a boat and explore it, can you, Granny?"

"I think we'll save that pleasure for another day if you don't mind. All I want at this moment is a nice hot cup of tea. Let's find that dog of yours and *then* maybe we can find the café."

Granny waited, sitting on a low wall, while Fred ran a short way along the path and disappeared round a bend, following the sound of frantic barking.

He was back almost immediately, holding on tightly to Monty's collar.

"Come on Granny!" he shouted. "There's a posh looking hotel just round that bend. I'm sure we'll be able to get you a cup of tea there."

# Chapter 6

Posh was the word! Fred had never seen anything like it before. The hotel had been painted a dazzling white colour and it was *huge*. He put his head back and stared at a large sign that ran the whole width of the enormous building.

"The Clansman Hotel," he sounded out slowly. Then, "What's a Clansman?"

"Well now, Fred, a clan is a sort of tribe. If you could trace your family tree back far enough, you would find out that the Boggitts are related to the MacBoggitts. Braveheart MacBoggitt was *your* ancestor."

"Wow! But why aren't I called Fred MacBoggitt then? That would be truly spectacular."

"Because you're also related to Big Mac MacBoggitt and he did something so shocking, so frightfully awful that we don't ever mention him.

"What did he do?" Fred gasped.

"I don't know. But I just hope that the folks round here don't have long memories. I don't want a good holiday ruined by a nasty feud."

"What's a *fyood* Granny?"

"A *murderous attack* that's what," she whispered.

Fred gulped and stood rooted to the spot.

There were nine steps in front of them, flanked by stone lions and palms in large pots, leading up to sparkling glass doors.

"Come on then, Fred, hurry up. I hear that cup of tea calling."

"Won't it be a bit too expensive? I mean, I haven't been given my pocket money yet. Hey! That's a thought – it's still Saturday isn't it? Remind me to ask Dad."

But Granny was already almost sprinting up the stairs. When she arrived at the top, huffing and puffing, the doors opened as if by magic. Fred assumed that they were automatic. They had plenty of those in Slough. However, he soon discovered that he was wrong! Next to the door through which Granny was entering the hotel, was a revolving door. Fred hadn't seen many of those and the opportunity seemed too good to miss. It was on approximately his tenth revolution that one of the men, who had in fact opened the door for Granny, somehow managed to stop him mid-spin.

"Aw!" Fred said. "I was enjoying that!"

"And what can we do for you, Sonny Jim?" Mr. Spoilsport asked, in a kind of put-on-posh, Scottish voice. "If you want the Caravan and Campsite..."

Fred stared at him in disbelief. The man was dressed in a dark red uniform, with gold ribbon round the edges and tassels on his shoulders. He looked a bit like a soldier, but what was he doing holding doors open?

"He's with me," Granny said quickly, grabbing Fred's arm and looking down in surprise at the man's scruffy grey trainers. "We've come for a cup of tea."

"Well, we're not serving tea at the ..."

Just at that moment a small, thin man wearing a smart dark suit appeared and called out to them as he approached,

"Good afternoon to you both. My name is Dougal MacNoodle and I'm the hotel manager. Is it a cup of tea you're after?" He turned to one of the men in uniform. "Fergal here will show you through to the lounge and he'll see to it that you get a nice pot of tea for two, won't you Fergal?"

"Can I have a coke please mister?" Fred asked politely.

"I'm sure that can be arranged young man," the manager replied, glancing downwards and appearing to notice, for the first time, two sets of muddy footprints on his bright red carpet. He noticed, too, the mud that was caking the visitors' shoes and the way that Granny's pop socks were all wrinkly round her ankles.

"Um, would that be your dog I can hear barking, sir?"

Fred had forgotten Monty's lead, but on the spur of the moment he had come up with an inventive alternative. Rather cleverly, if he said so himself, he had decided on the idea of using the fluorescent green cord from his binoculars. He had managed to unfasten the few knots that secured it to the glasses and had threaded it through the dog's collar. Then he had attached the other end of the cord to the railings which ran round the flower beds next to the hotel's main entrance.

"It's all right," Granny assured the manager, "he'll quieten down in a minute."

With this, Mr. MacNoodle hurried off to find one of the cleaners, leaving Fergal to escort the two 'guests' to the lounge.

"Shove 'em in the library," Granny distinctly heard the other doorman, the one wearing glasses, the really, really tall one, whisper rather too loudly to Fergal.

"Aye, I'll do that Hamish," Fergal replied, hurrying to catch up with Granny who had set off down the corridor at a lick. "There won't be much in the form of a tip from those two."

"The library!" Fergal announced a few seconds later, pointing to a dimly lit room, not much bigger than a broom cupboard. Granny managed to spot one rather tattered magazine resting on a stool, before turning sharply to her left.

"This will do very nicely," she said, marching into the lounge, closely followed by her grandson.

"You can't go in there - there's no room!" Fergal replied, so loudly that the forty pairs of eyes belonging to the other occupants of the room swivelled in horror to stare at him.

"Oh, I'm sure this nice man here won't mind budging up, will you sir?" Granny said. "We're only small... well, Fred is! And I'd like plenty of sugar with my tea," she called across the room to the rapidly disappearing Fergal.

Granny took off her poncho and placed it carefully over the back of the settee.

"My name is Gordon Campbell," the old gentleman said in a jolly kind of way, as Granny squeezed in next to him. "I see you're wearing a kilt. Those colours are rather unusual if I may say so. I don't think I've seen them before."

"I'm glad you like it. I had it made specially to come to Scotland. The colours – shocking pink and lime green - are the colours of our ancestors. This is our own special tartan. My name's Florence Boggitt by the way. Known as Florrie to my friends and I'm pleased to make your acquaintance. And this young man is my grandson, Freddie."

"How do you do?" Fred said, in his poshest voice. "We're staying at the Piece of Carrot Campsite."

"He means the Bit of Peace and Quiet Campsite," Granny explained quickly.

Fred found a stool to sit on and began exploring the loch through his binoculars.

The whole of one wall of the lounge was entirely made of glass so that the view of the loch seemed to be a part of the room itself.

"It's spectacular!" he breathed.

By this time the tea and coke had arrived, brought by a very smiley faced waitress dressed in a black and white uniform and wearing white gloves.

"Shall I pour?" she asked, as she put the tray down.

"Oo, yes please," Granny said. "And those shortbread biscuits look nice," she added, eyeing the biscuits on Mr. Campbell's plate.

"Please help yourself." He glanced across at Fred. "The wee laddie seems to be enjoying the view."

"Oh, he is. But what he really wants is to catch a glimpse of the Loch Ness Monster," Granny remarked, munching away.

"Well, he's come to the right place."

"What d'you mean?" Fred asked, swivelling round on his seat, his eyes as big as car hub caps. "Don't tell me you've seen it?"

"I most certainly have," Mr. Campbell announced, leaning forwards. "Nessie we call her."

"And *I've* seen her," a lady in a seat nearby called out.

"And me."

"And me."

"I have too."

It soon became clear that every single person who was seated in the lounge had seen 'Nessie' at least once. Some of them had even seen her as many as three times.

"This is amazing," Fred said. "It's wicked. Spectacular even!"

"We *all* saw her just the other day. It was on Monday, actually. The twelfth of April. I remember the date so well because it's our wedding anniversary," Mr. Campbell stated, smiling across at his wife and clearly quite pleased to have such an interested audience, for once. "It was after tea and we were all lined up, sipping a spot of sherry before dinner, don't you know, when all at once Brenda over there..."

"It wasn't Brenda, it was Morag," a voice from the other side of the room interrupted.

"All right then, when *Morag* suddenly yelled, "Aaaaah! The Monster – it's right there in the middle of the lake." She was so shocked that she spilt most of her sherry. A good one it was too!"

"I can tell ye it was the most frightening thing that's ever happened to me!" Morag said, taking over the story. "The sun was just setting, sort of spooky like, and the mist was swirling about like in those horror movies, when all of a sudden this terrible great beastie appeared in front of ma very own eyes. And, what's more, it just sat there staring at me with its great, glinting, evil ..."

"Well it didn't actually, Morag," someone else spoke from the opposite side of the room. "It sort of sailed to and fro for a wee while and then it swam round and round in circles, before disappearing into the weeds. Although I have to agree it *was* terrifying. I loved it!"

"There you go then Fred. There's proof that the Loch Ness Monster *does* exist. That's something to tell your dad," Granny remarked, her eyes sparkling and her cheeks glowing.

Just then, as if on cue, the theme from 'Jaws' echoed round the room. The guests looked startled, stopped talking at once and turned to look at the loch.

"Er, my mobile," Granny apologised, reaching into her handbag.

"Um, yes. Yes. Yes, Fred senior. We're having a lovely time. We're sitting in the lounge of this posh hotel at the moment. I said we're sitting... Yes. Well some of them are a bit stuck up but the others are all right. Yes we've had a cup of tea and a biscuit. The shortbread isn't as good as mine though. Right, well, I'd better go then. See you later."

Fred was sitting quietly, sipping his coke and making notes in his little red book, all the while keeping one eye on the water in case the Monster should obligingly appear.

"He writes everything down, our Fred does," Granny said proudly, popping her mobile back into her bag.

After that, unfortunately, there was very little opportunity for conversation. Somewhere close by a piano had struck up and a man was singing, at the top of his voice, a song that sounded a bit like, "Donald where's ya trousers?"

It was difficult to tell really, partly because the man's Scottish accent was so strong, but mainly because from somewhere outside the hotel was coming the most awful howling sound.

# Chapter 7

By the time Fred and Granny returned to the campsite the tent was up, at least it *looked* as if it was up – well almost. It was beginning to get dark as they battled their way up a fairly steep slope, fighting a wind which seemed determined to blow them over. Even the stumpy trees and bushes were bending sideways and their smudgy silhouettes looked sort of eerie and menacing.

Fred was very relieved to reach his temporary home and he found himself running up to the tent, where he pretended to knock on the door.

"Knock, knock! It's us!" he called.

"Is anybody in?" Granny asked, chuckling.

A hand unzipped the tent flap and Mr. Boggitt's head peered out, like a rabbit out of a hat. Monty immediately barged past him, his tail thrashing about madly from side to side and connecting with one of the supporting poles, which shuddered with the impact.

"Watch out Monty, you stupid dog!" Mr. Boggitt bellowed. Then, "Come in, come in," he said. "We wondered where you'd got to. We were beginning to get worried, weren't we Mother? Well, we're very cosy in here, I must say."

Fred didn't think his dad *did* look very cosy as a matter of fact. For a start, his hair was standing up on end, held in position by a rampant south-easterly which was ripping through the tent. As he stepped inside, Fred spotted a large piece of canvas flapping about where it had escaped from the peg that was meant to be keeping it in place.

"I can't seem to find the spare tent pegs. I'm sure I packed them," a puzzled Mr. Boggitt muttered.

"A bit elusive are they Dad?" Fred asked innocently.

"I hope you checked for ants' nests," Granny said, ducking down and crawling inside. "Only I got bitten half to death last time. Here! This tent's a bit wonky isn't it?" she added, peering around in the gloom.

"Oh, don't you start!" Mr. Boggitt snapped. He was sitting on a small, canvas, fold-up chair with a plastic cup of what smelled like coffee in his hand. For some reason he was wearing a bright green jumper with only one sleeve. "I've had Mr. Know-it-all Melvyn what's-'is-name from across the way giving me the benefit of his advice for the past three hours."

"Two and three quarters, actually," Mrs. Boggitt corrected him. "And he did make you that nice cup of coffee when he saw that you were having no success with lighting the stove." She looked across at her husband and shook her head. "He was only trying to help."

"Only trying to help my foot! "You did remember to clear the earth of stones before you put the ground sheet down, didn't you?"" he mimicked. "And, "You have colour-coded your tent poles so you know which one goes where, haven't you?" I'd like to have colour-coded him with my mallet, I can tell you."

"Sit down you two. You're making the place look untidy," Mrs. Boggitt joked. "Oh, Fred, put that dog in its basket first will you? It's making me itch, forever scratching itself. And don't take any notice of your father. He's just a bit tired."

"And then he starts to tell me which way round to put the sleeping bags! The nerve of the man. As if I can't arrange my own bedroom furniture."

"Right! That's enough now! Since it's too windy to light the stove, I'm going to go and fetch us all some nice fish and chips from the café. Come on Monty. You can come with me and maybe that'll stop you scratching for a few minutes. And perhaps when your Dad's had his dinner he'll be in a bit better mood. Then, Fred, you and Granny can tell us what you've been up to this afternoon."

"I think I saw the Monster, Mum. Everyone says it's got humps and I definitely saw three humps sticking up out of the water."

"Those were rocks, Freddie. I keep trying to tell you. They weren't moving. Monsters move,"

Granny said patiently. "I must say though, Fred senior, this is all very nice. You've made it feel quite homely with those plastic flowers and the candlesticks. It reminds me of when I used to go camping with the Brownies."

"You were a Brownie?" Fred spluttered, not quite able to imagine it.

"Yes I was," Granny replied indignantly, "and a Girl Guide after that. It was good fun. You should try it."

"I would, but don't you have to be a girl?"

"Ha ha! Very funny!"

Mrs. Boggitt began rummaging in her handbag for her purse.

"Dad," Fred said. "Can I ask you a question? Is it my imagination or has the tent just moved? Only Granny was sitting in the middle of it a minute ago and now she's on the edge with the canvas resting on her head."

# Chapter 8

After they had eaten their fish and chips and washed them down with fairly cold tea drunk from paper cups, everyone did indeed feel much better.

"Fish and chips always taste so much better straight from the paper - and there's no washing up either," Mrs. Boggitt remarked, screwing her greasy bag into a ball and tossing it into a black rubbish sack.

"We'll have to sort out a recycling container tomorrow," Mr. Boggitt said, tilting back rather dangerously in his chair. "We can't let our standards slip just because we're on holiday."

Even Monty had settled down in his basket, after a snack of tinned sardines, a couple of 'Chewies' and a few chips more than were good for him.

For the time being it didn't seem to matter that the whole tent smelled fishy, that the ground felt lumpy and uneven so that their chairs wobbled, and that the roof was much lower in some places than others, so that they had to duck their heads whenever they moved about. And, as Mrs. Boggitt rightly remarked, the wind which blew in through the gaps where a couple of tent pegs had 'pinged' themselves out of the ground, only served to air the sleeping bags, which were a bit musty having not been used for a good few years.

"Go on then, Fred," Mrs. Boggitt said as she served pudding – two Jaffa cakes each and a finger of Kit-Kat – "tell us all about this fancy hotel you say you went to."

"It was well posh, Mum," Fred said. "You would have loved it, wouldn't she Granny? There were great big stags' heads on the walls and some of the biggest fish I've ever seen. They looked ginormous through my binoculars."

"It was all right, I suppose," Granny said. "Just don't ask me how much I paid for a pot of tea and a coke. I thought they'd given me their electricity bill by mistake."

"And loads of people who were staying there had seen the Loch Ness Monster, Dad. I wrote most of it down in my book, what they said and everything."

"Fred, I've told you, the Monster doesn't exist, any more than the Abominable Snowman does, or Big Foot, or Big Ears for that matter," Mr. Boggitt declared. "And I don't want to hear you going on about it any more. Do you understand me? Just relax and enjoy yourself!"

"But Dad..." Fred protested.

"No, not another word on the subject. And I don't care how posh that hotel of yours is, nothing can beat this tent for comfort and style. There's nothing like the feeling you get when you're sleeping out in the open, under canvas and..." (Here Mr. Boggitt had to pause suddenly in order to take a swipe at a couple of midges that were bobbing up and down on his bare right arm) "...and the joy you experience... SLAP... just knowing ...SLAP, SLAP ... that you are at one ...SLAP, SLAP, SLAP... with Mother Nature."

By the time he had finished speaking, the whole tent had been invaded by busy, biting little midges and he was having to rush to his rucksack.

"Ah ha!" he shouted after a brief rummage, running round the tent emptying the contents of an aerosol into the atmosphere. "Midge repellent! That should do the trick!"

"Boggitt repellent you mean," Granny coughed. "You're only supposed to give a few squirts, not use up the whole can! Anyway, I'm off to my bed, where the air will be a whole lot sweeter. Come on Fred, it's been a long old day."

# Chapter 9

It might have been a long day, but it proved to be an even longer night – at least for Fred, who was sharing a room with Granny. It had been fun, at first, getting ready for bed by the thin, watery beam of his little wind-up torch and rinsing his mouth, after brushing his teeth, with only a beaker of water and a bucket.

He could hear his father singing, "There was a wee cooper who lived in Fife, nicketty, nacketty, noo, noo, noo," next door and he smiled to himself as he helped Granny into her sleeping bag and zipped her in.

"I feel like an Egyptian mummy," she chuckled. "There's not much room to move, is there?"

"Keep you warm," Fred replied, trying to balance his torch on the steeply tilted ground, close to his own sleeping bag. Next he set his new alarm clock. "I'll set it to go off nice and early. We don't want to be late getting up."

"If you say so dear. Goodnight Freddie. God bless."

"Goodnight Granny. Sleep tight."

Before he could go to sleep, Fred had a couple of things to jot down in his notebook. He picked up his wind-up torch. Two minutes of winding would give him thirty minutes of light, the instructions said. He needed about ten minutes, so that would mean he'd have to wind the handle for ...um! That was a tricky one. In any case, he still had some light left, so it didn't really matter. He decided to give it a few winds for luck, but then Granny complained about what she thought was a bluebottle in the tent so he gave up.

As it happened, he just managed to write down what he remembered of Morag's sighting of the Loch Ness Monster, especially what she'd said about it being 'a terrible great beastie', and the date of its appearance, when the blue light of the torch flickered and went out.

Even without the glow of the torch it wasn't as dark as you might think in the tent. There was a full moon, even though its light seemed to click on and off as one cloud after another scudded across it. It was like trying to sleep next to a lighthouse. The wind was whining and whistling too, far louder now than when they had all been sitting together eating. And when it started howling, it sounded like a were-wolf, making the hairs on the back of Fred's neck stand on end. Added to all that, the tent was creaking and flapping, giving the strong impression that it was about to collapse on top of them at any moment.

Fred tried pulling the sleeping bag up over his head. He screwed his eyes up and put his fingers in his ears, but it did no good.

His nerves were stretched as tightly as the guy ropes *should* have been, so it is no wonder that he nearly jumped out of his skin when, a few seconds later, he heard a strange-sounding voice calling across to him,

"Fred, are you asleep? Only I'm dot. My dose is all blocked up."

Fred breathed a sigh of relief then peered over the edge of his sleeping bag. The floor of this part of the tent was on a particularly steep slope. His bed was tilted sharply and so too was Granny's, so that it was a bit like trying to get to sleep fastened to the side of Mount Everest. He noticed that Granny's nose was squashed up against the side of the tent, too, and all at once he remembered something his dad had said. He slipped out of bed and carefully manoeuvred her round the other way so that the blood would run to her feet instead of her head and her nose would be away from the canvas wall.

Then he hopped back into bed.

Would you believe it? There were other noises now, coming from just outside the tent - sort of snuffling, mooing, bleating, hooting, squeaking sounds. Fred suddenly wondered where Monty was.

"Fred? Fred! I've got indigestion," Granny wailed loudly, making him jump yet again. "Oh!" she groaned in agony, "it was the batter on those fish and chips. It always gives me indigestion. Only I can't get to my tablets because I can't move my arms."

Fred heaved a sigh and clambered out of his sleeping bag, stubbing his big toe on one of the tent poles as he did so. It took him several minutes to locate the packet of 'Burp Easy' pills, because Granny's handbag was like a small suitcase and stocked with more medicines than their local chemist.

"Open wide," Fred said eventually, and flicked a tablet into her mouth.

He was so tired that he practically sleep-walked back to his bed, yawning loudly all the way. This time the nylon of his sleeping bag felt especially cold against his chilly body. For what seemed like ages, he tried not to think about it and go to sleep, but, by now, of course, he was feeling all too wide awake. And every time the wind pounded the tent, he could hear a popping – pinging sort of sound. He couldn't imagine what it was.

"Fred!" came Granny's voice for the third time.

"What is it now?" he called back impatiently. "I'm trying to get some sleep!"

"And so am I, but it's rather difficult when your sleeping bag is resting on a couple of pine cones as big as dinosaur eggs and you're sharing it with a nest of biting ants."

Fred groaned. He was about to scramble out of bed, for the third time, when he became aware of yet another noise. It sounded like workmen digging up the road, but it was, in fact, just the sound of Granny snoring.

After that, Fred remained well and truly awake for the rest of the night. He didn't mind the moonlight or the dark, spindly shapes that moved across the canvas walls. He could cope with all of that. He could shut his eyes. It was the wind he hated. How much longer 'til morning, he wondered. He couldn't see what time it was. His alarm clock had blown over. But then, just as the first bird – the early riser – began to tweet its welcome to the new day, the wind dropped at last, but not before it managed one last almighty blast that blew the tent away.

# Chapter 10

"Well that's very annoying, I must say," Mr. Boggitt said a few seconds later, as he found himself staring across at Fred and Granny, who were peering out of their sleeping bags like startled ferrets. "The tent's blown away! Now how did that happen, I wonder?"

Mrs. Boggitt suddenly screamed an ear-splitting scream.

"Aaaah! Granny what's happened to your face?"

Fred giggled. "She asked me to put a stocking over her head to stop the midges from biting," he explained.

"Good heavens. I had the fright of my life. I thought she'd been hit on the head with a flying tent pole. Fred, will you tell that mad dog of yours to stop howling like that. It's not helping."

"The tent should never have blown away like that, Mother," Mr. Boggitt remarked, scratching his head. "The man who sold it to me *said* it was wind proof. And just when I was in the middle of a nice dream too. Anyway, I suppose we'd better put some clothes on and go and look for it."

But Fred was already dressed. He had called to Monty and then snatched up his binoculars and was busily peering over the hedge, next to where he had been trying to sleep 'under canvas' – up until ten minutes ago. The wind had dropped all right, but it been blowing towards the loch, so the chances were that the tent was somewhere to the right of them.

"It'll be miles away by now," Mr. Boggitt called, running over to join his son a few minutes later. "Trust me; it'll have flown like a kite."

"No, I can see it Dad."

"Where son, where are we looking?"

"Right over there," Fred said, pointing to a large, green object in the middle of the field next to them. There were a few black and white cows at the far side of the field, busily munching on grass and turning it into gold tops. They didn't seem bothered by a flying carpet made of canvas.

"Oh well, that's no problem," Mr. Boggitt said matter-of-factly, finally spying the stray tent and trying to squeeze himself through the hedge. There was a loud ripping sound as one of the toggles on his duffle coat caught on the spiky twigs of the hedge and stuck firm, whilst the rest of him barged on.

"Bother!" he said, but a few seconds later, having left half his coat behind, he was lumbering across the field. Monty followed, his woolly ears flapping and his pink tongue lolling out of the side of his mouth, to where the tent, or what was left of it, was draped limply over a large, prickly bush. The dog ran round and round it, in a frenzy of excitement, his barking reaching fever pitch.

"BE QUIET!" Mr. Boggitt commanded, just as he'd seen the experts do on T.V., but with absolutely no success. "You'll wake everybody up. Now SIT!"

But Monty was having far too much fun. Grabbing the canvas between his sharp little teeth, he began pulling it with all his might, anchoring his four paws securely to the ground and tossing his head from side to side, all the while making excited growling noises deep in his throat.

"Do you want some help, Dad?" Fred shouted, as his father began trying to disentangle the shredded green canvas from the both the bush *and* from Monty.

"It seems to be stuck," Granny shouted, rather unnecessarily.

But after some frantic tugging, a few angry tearing sounds could be heard and the bush suddenly released its hold on the tent, so that Mr. Boggitt was catapulted backwards.

"Be careful, Fred senior," Mrs. Boggitt called, just several seconds too late.

Mr. Boggitt, huffing and puffing angrily, picked himself up from the ground and gathered the material to him as well as he could. He began hurrying across the grass, back to where his family stood anxiously at the hedge, tripping over dangling bits of canvas, and the dog, which refused to let go, as he went. And there he stood, catching his breath and looking very red in the face, on the other side of the hedge.

"Watch out for the bulls, Dad," Fred warned.

"They're not *bulls* Fred. They're cows. Don't you know anything?" Mr. Boggitt snapped bad-temperedly.

"I think the boy's right, Fred senior. One of those 'cows' is a bull," Granny said.

"I'd get out of there quick, if I were you," Mrs. Boggitt advised.

Mr. Boggitt was about to tell them what he thought of their advice when he noticed the expressions of horror that had appeared on all three faces at exactly the same moment. He turned briefly to look. Behind him, an enormous, fierce-looking, black bull - one of Scotland's finest - was pawing the ground with one mighty hoof, his bloodshot eyes rolling in his head and white clouds pouring from his fiery nostrils.

One quick look was all it took. One second Mr. Boggitt was standing squarely on Scottish earth, the next he was hurtling towards them at a hundred miles an hour. When he reached the hedge he shot up into the air, just as if he'd been shot from a cannon, so that he cleared it by half a mile. The dog was only a fraction of a second behind him.

The rest of the Boggitts clapped and whistled in admiration.

"Wow Dad!" Fred exclaimed. "You probably just broke the world record with that jump."

"That was a close thing," Mr. Boggitt gasped, as his knees buckled under him and he collapsed in a heap on the ground. "I can still feel that bull's hot breath on the back of my legs."

# Chapter 11

It took Mr. Boggitt several minutes to calm down after this narrowest of escapes, but at last he pulled himself together. He stared for a time at their scattered belongings, while scratching his head and mumbling to himself.

It was very quiet on the campsite. No one seemed to be stirring. Of course, it was very early in the morning and it was obvious that all the other campers were still asleep. Even the birds were silent for the time being.

The Boggitts, apart from Mr. Boggitt that is, were sitting in a circle on their fold-up chairs. In the middle of the floor, in a torn and tangled mess, the remains of the tent were strewn.

Mr. Boggitt pulled one of the chairs towards him with his foot and then opened his mouth to speak. But before he could sit down or utter one word, the peace was shattered by an ear-splitting whooping sound that reverberated round the field. It was the sort of noise a hen might make having laid a few cube-shaped eggs.

At once, heads appeared at the flaps of the other tents and angry voices yelled across the field.

"'Ere! What's going on?"

"Do you know what time it is?"

"Put a sock in it will you!"

"Shut it or else..."

"Turn that rotten thing off before I come and..."

"Who? What?" Mr. Boggitt spluttered.

"Sorry Dad," Fred muttered, throwing himself off his chair and frantically scrabbling around on the floor. "My new alarm clock," he explained, as he picked it up from the floor and began fiddling with a series of switches, trying to find the right one.

"Fred you nearly gave me and your Granny a heart attack!" Mrs. Boggitt wailed, clutching her throat.

"They used to have sirens like that in the war. Nearly frightened me to death," Granny moaned.

"Right, well, now that the excitement's over, I suggest we get down to business," Mr. Boggitt said, mopping his forehead with his hankie. "We have urgent matters to discuss. Firstly the matter of the tent..."

"I don't think it's going to be much use to us now, Dad."

"No, I think that's rather obvious, Fred," Mr. Boggitt agreed, holding the sorry-looking piece of canvas up for examination. "I phoned the man who sold it to me. Got him out of bed. I gave him a piece of my mind, I can tell you. He assured me that the tent *was* in fact wind-proof, but wasn't designed to be used when the wind was actually blowing."

"And did he say whether or not it was hole-proof? Because it's more hole than tent, if you ask me," Granny said. "Just look at those big tears in it. I wonder what it was did that."

Fred's eyes began to sparkle.

"You don't suppose..."

"No, I don't Fred Boggitt," his dad interrupted. "And you'd better not suppose either, if you're thinking what I think you're thinking. It was bushes, and wind, and bulls made the tears, not a monster that nobody's seen..."

"But Dad..."

"As I was saying, your mother and I are going to Inverness today to see your Auntie Ethel in her new guest house. You can come with us if you want to Fred. And while we're there, we'll see about getting a new tent - one that works this time!"

"Aw, Dad, do I have to? I came to see the Loch Ness Mon... er, Loch Ness. Can't Granny stay and look after me? Please?"

"Has it occurred to you, Fred, that Granny might want to see...?"

"You sort out your own arrangements," Mr. Boggitt interrupted wearily. "And may I suggest that everybody wears white clothing today." He picked up a huge, well-worn book from the ground entitled 'The Campers' Bible'. "It says in here that midges hate white. Good! They hate garlic too, so I'll be cooking with plenty of that tonight, rest assured. And now I'm going to get breakfast on the go. I'm hungry, I don't know about anybody else."

# Chapter 12

After this latest 'briefing', Mrs. Boggitt, Fred and Granny made their way over to the campsite's shower block to get cleaned up. They left Mr. Boggitt alone to start cooking the breakfast – at his request.

Since nobody else seemed to be up yet, there was no queue, so it wasn't long before they appeared back at their site, one after the other, all gleaming whitely like an advert for clothes washing capsules.

Amazingly, the smell of burned sausages that greeted them on their return, made them smack their lips as if they had only just realised how hungry they were.

"That smells good, Fred senior," Mrs. Boggitt called to her husband. "Almost good enough to eat," she joked.

"You set the table, Mother, and we'll be ready in a jiffy," Mr. Boggitt said, smiling to himself. "We may not have a tent, but we still have standards to maintain."

"I'm starving!" Fred shouted from half way across the field. "Can I make mine into a sandwich?"

"Yuck!" said Granny. "You've burnt the sausages again. Don't give me any. I'd rather be shot than poisoned. The dog can have 'em."

"Suit yourself," Mr. Boggitt replied, trying not to sound too put out. "But there's nothing wrong with my cooking. And in case you haven't noticed, I have treated us to a new, multi-burner stove with added extras: push button ignition, adjustable flame and wind shield. Clever, eh?" he said, demonstrating each function with a flourish.

"I hope you remembered to bring extra gas canisters, Fred senior..." Mrs. Boggitt said.

"Er!"

"...not like that last time. Do you remember, you forgot to bring spare canisters and we couldn't buy any anywhere and..."

"I know. I was there," Mr. Boggitt said waspishly, going very red in the face.

Just then a voice yelled to them from one of the other tents.

"I hope you've noticed that big tree there, folks. Only that large branch is rather close to your stove. I'd hate it to catch fire."

"Yes, thank you very much for the warning, Melvyn," Mr. Boggitt said irritably, brandishing a hot spatula dangerously.

"Mervyn," the voice replied. "The name's Mervyn. I was sorry to hear about your tent blowing away like that, by the way. Still, if there's anything I can do? I've got plenty of spare tent pegs if you need them. You've only got to say."

"Thank you for the offer. We'll be sure to ask you," Mrs. Boggitt replied quickly, before her husband had the chance to do anything he might be sorry for later.

"And, if you don't mind me making a little suggestion," Mervyn added, "since the wind's blowing from the south-west today, why don't you turn your wind shield round, like so. That way your flame won't keep going out."

# Chapter 13

After they finished eating, and had washed up and cleared away, Mr. and Mrs. Boggitt said their farewells and set off to Inverness to see Auntie Ethel. Granny had agreed to spend the day with Fred. She would go and see her sister another day.

"Look after Granny, Fred, and be a good boy. And don't let that daft dog annoy anyone," Mrs. Boggitt called merrily, staggering across the field in her rather tight white trousers and top, and her high heeled shoes. "We'll be back about five."

"And don't leave any valuables on display. We've got to think about security until we get another tent," Mr. Boggitt shouted, running backwards. He was still yelling instructions to them when he reached the car park, but by that time they couldn't hear a word he was saying.

"Oh well," Granny said, picking up her umbrella. "It can't have been that important. And I hope his wallet isn't either. He's left it here on his chair."

"Mum'll have money," Fred said, picking up his carrying case and stuffing his binoculars, torch, timer, compass and alarm clock inside. "Come on Monty. But be warned, as soon as we get to the loch you're going on your lead."

It was a much better day today. The sun was peeping out from behind a few low, fluffy white clouds and there was already the hint of warmth in the air.

The path down to Loch Ness was much drier than it had been the day before, except in those sheltered places where the wind hadn't been able to reach it to dry it out. The ground was littered with small twigs and bigger branches, which the wind had ripped off during the night, and they cracked and splintered under their feet as they walked.

From one of the trees, high above their heads came a sharp tapping sound. Fred stopped and looked up in surprise.

"What's that Granny?" he asked, frowning. "It's not a rattle snake is it?"

"No," Granny laughed. "It's a woodpecker. Only I can't see it can you? You don't tend to find many rattle snakes in Britain. And talking about things that are hard to spot, where's that Monty got to?"

Fred called, not seriously expecting any response, which was just as well, for he got none. He tried whistling.

By this time, they had nearly reached the loch and the trees were beginning to thin out a little. From somewhere to their left came a loud rustling noise. They weren't too surprised as they'd heard warblings and flutterings coming from the undergrowth all the way down, but there was something rather familiar about this particular sound.

Granny pulled back some low-hanging branches with her umbrella whilst Fred investigated. There stood Monty, staring back at them with a look of guilty triumph on his face, frantically wagging his tail. Something was dangling limply from his mouth.

"What have you got now?" Fred asked uncertainly. Monty had brought many disgusting things to his owner in the past and experience had taught Fred to be very wary. "How you don't die of poisoning I'll never know," he murmured, grabbing hold of the latest piece of treasure.

This time, however, even though Monty was very reluctant to let go, his 'find' turned out to be nothing more exciting than a tattered piece of grey and green material.

"What's he got now?" Granny asked, peering over the top of her glasses.

Fred shrugged. Then he felt himself going very cold all over. "It's ... it's not a piece of ... skin, is it?" he gulped.

"Don't be silly," Granny said, snatching the piece of material from him and examining it more closely. "It's a piece of that camouflage stuff they make jackets from. You should know, you used to have one didn't you?" But she knew as she spoke that what she was saying wasn't right. The material felt too rubbery to be clothing. It felt too cold and thin, somehow ... and sort of scaly.

# Chapter 14

"Can we go on a boat trip, please Granny?" Fred asked, as he pulled Monty away from the water's edge and attached his lead.

They walked over to a large blackboard that had a list of all the day's sailings.

"The first boat leaves in half an hour," Granny said, squinting at her watch. "We're the first ones here. Let's sit on that bench and wait."

The boat was called 'Pride of the Glen' and even though it looked spotlessly clean, two men were busily washing the paintwork and polishing the already gleaming windows.

Fred was peering through his binoculars, turning his head this way and that every time something new caught his attention. As he watched, the whole of the loch seemed to be springing to life. It was going to be a fine day and people were here to enjoy themselves.

"Can we sit outside, please?" Fred asked, as they boarded the boat at last, and Granny handed over the money for the tickets.

They had been the first to arrive at the little landing stage, but they suddenly found themselves at the back of rather a large queue. However, Granny showed no hesitation in pushing to the front.

"We were here first," she said, and made her way to the front of the boat, ignoring the mutterings of the other passengers.

"Sassenach!" someone called after her.

"Bless you!" Granny replied.

The owner of the boat was a small man with a large red beard and bushy eyebrows. He was wearing a red and green tartan hat on his head, with a bobble on the top.

"My name is Hector MacDougal and I'm the owner of this boat and this is my son, Robbie. We'd like to welcome you aboard. I'll ask you to keep that wee dog of yours on a tight lead young laddie," he called to Fred. "I'll no be diving in to rescue him if he falls overboard, nor you neither."

Fred glanced at Granny and then tied Monty's lead firmly to the railings. The dog seemed happy enough as he leaned his head forwards and began sniffing the air.

Once they were all aboard, the boat cast away from its moorings and chugged into the loch.

The surface of the water was much calmer today, but there was still a fairly stiff breeze blowing that they hadn't really noticed on land.

Granny felt a drop of water land on her face and made to put up her umbrella.

"I wouldna be doing that in this wind if I were you," Hector MacDougal, called out. "You'll be finding yerself flying over the loch like Mary Poppins. Yon steep banks turn the loch into a regular wind funnel, they do that. And, by the way, that was spray ye felt, not rain."

As the boat headed away from the landing stage, Fred turned his head and looked along the shoreline through his binoculars.

"There's the hotel we went to yesterday – The Clansman," he said, pointing it out to Granny. "It looks even bigger from here doesn't it?"

But Granny had no chance to reply because at that moment the boat's owner began talking to them over the loud speaker.

"Loch Ness is one of four lochs that link together with..."

Some people carried on talking, ignoring the commentary that Mr. MacDougal was providing, as they cruised over the water. This made it quite difficult for those who *did* want to listen to hear what he was saying. Granny tried saying, "Shush!" loudly a few times but no one seemed to take any notice.

"The loch itself is one mile wide and..."

"I knew that. I told you that Freddie," Granny shouted.

"Shush!" someone behind her said. "We're trying to hear what the man's got to say."

"Hey!" a woman sitting to the left of them called. "Little boy, tell your dog to stop licking my leg. Ugh! You horrible creature!"

"Don't you talk to my grandson like that!" Granny said, pointing her finger and glaring at the woman.

"And he's just eaten my son's crisps," another woman said.

"...fishing for sea trout and salmon. It's a wee bit early but..." Mr. MacDougal was saying.

Fred searched frantically round the deck for Monty, but there was no sign of him. Finding that his lead would slide easily along the slippery metal railing, the dog had quickly made his way to the stern of the boat, where he was busily licking someone's ice cream off the deck. Fred hurried to fetch him and decided to keep hold of his lead to prevent any more problems.

"Hey, wee laddie!" a voice shouted from somewhere behind him.

Fred gulped and turned round. It was the owner of the boat calling him. Had someone complained to him about the dog, he wondered.

"Hey! Would you like to come and steer the boat?"

Wouldn't he just? Passing Monty's lead to Granny, he hurried to where Mr. MacDougal stood waiting for him to take control.

"Thanks, Mister," Fred said in his politest voice and began turning the wheel enthusiastically from side to side.

"Whoa there, laddie. Gently does it, like so."

While Freddie *carefully* steered the boat, Mr. MacDougal carried on with his commentary. His passengers continued to chat to each other, so that, at last, he sighed and gave up.

"I'll let you enjoy the rest of the trip in peace," he said.

# Chapter 15

Soon it was someone else's turn to steer the boat. Fred thanked the owner and went to sit back down. Now that Mr. MacDougal had stopped speaking, everybody had gone quiet.

Monty had slipped under one of the seats and fallen asleep, and so had Granny. (Well, she hadn't actually slipped under the seat, but she *had* fallen asleep.) Fred rested his chin on the cold railing and stared at the scenery.

He was quite used to being near water. He went fishing with his dad most week-ends. The river where they fished was very different to this loch, though. *His* river was shallow and the water was so clear that he could easily see the pebbles on the river bed. And even though most of the fish in it were expertly camouflaged, if you watched really carefully you could often make out their pale, freckled shapes weaving about.

Here it was different though. At the sides of the lake the water looked blue, mirroring the sky as you'd expect it to do. He could see reflections of pale houses on the surface, too, and the bright green trees, but nearer to the middle, where he was now, the water was a very dark green-grey colour. It was difficult to make out any shapes at all through it and absolutely impossible to see down to the bottom, no matter how hard he tried.

He said as much to Mr. MacDougal as he suddenly appeared at Fred's side.

"Och aye," Mr. MacDougal said in reply. "The water here is very deep and dark. Whatever secret the loch holds, she keeps it to herself."

"What do you mean?" Fred asked, lifting his head from the railing and turning his head to look at him.

"Why, there's only one mystery surrounding *this* loch and everyone knows what that is."

He glanced round at his passengers. "Hardly anyone listens when I give ma little talk. Oh, I know that all right. But you watch how they jump every time a ripple slaps the hull of my boat. They hear that just fine. They're on edge because they think they're about to come face to face with Nessie. And if I was to suddenly point my finger and yell, "Quick, look over there!" they'd listen to that too. Then the binoculars would be out and the cameras would be flashing. And that's the truth."

"Has that happened, then?" Fred asked, wondering if he should make a few notes in his book. "Has Nessie *acksherly* appeared?"

"Och no. I'm talking about *pretending*, laddie. Some people can't take a joke, ye ken, but I know right well what would happen."

"My dad says that the Loch Ness Monster doesn't exist. He says that people just imagine they've seen it. He says it's a bit like when you're in the desert and you *think* you see water."

"It's called a mirage," Mr. MacDougal said.

"Yes, one of those." Fred agreed, sucking the end of his pencil thoughtfully.

"People say all sorts of things," Mr. MacDougal said, staring out across the loch, "especially those folk who don't believe in Nessie. 'It was a log you saw floating on the water, or an otter,' they say. I ask you!"

"Surely anyone can tell the difference between a little old otter and an enormous monster!" Fred exclaimed, shaking his head.

"And, you know, there's an awful lot of water in Loch Ness. Why, it's as deep as the North Sea in places and the bottom is a maze of underwater caves and undiscovered channels leading to the sea. There are plenty of places for a creature to hide. Some experts think that Nessie might actually be a giant newt."

"*A giant newt!*" Fred repeated in astonishment, feeling excited now. "I saw a film once where the most ginormous octopus came out of the sea and knocked a boat over and everything! Do you think a giant newt might come out of the loch and do the same to us? That would be spectacular!"

"Or it might be a huge fish called a sturgeon that got blown off course..."

"We had a whale in the River Thames one day and it..."

"And what do *you* think, sir?" a voice interrupted from the other side of the boat. "Do you think it could actually be a plesiosaur left over from the dinosaur age?"

"Could you spell that please – that word you just used," Fred said eagerly, trying, but not really succeeding in recording the conversation on paper.

"Let me finish, laddie, and then I'll help you with your spelling. All right?" Mr. MacDougal looked at the other passengers, who were actually listening to him, for once.

"I'm afraid I don't know the answer to that question, but I'd be happy to tell you what I *do* know. Now it's a fact that there are hundreds of undiscovered wrecks scattered all over the bottom of the seas and oceans..."

"Like the Mary Rose was until a few years ago. I've been to see it in Portsmouth," Fred added enthusiastically. "My Granny took me."

"As I was trying to explain, these wrecks are *undiscovered*. Well now, if experts can't find the hundreds of wrecks that lay on the sea bed, and *they* stay *still*, why should we be surprised that they can't find one monster that moves about?"

"I don't get it," Fred said, scratching his head. "If they're *undiscovered* how do you know...?"

But the man sitting next to him wasn't listening. He was too busy thinking over what the captain of the boat had just said.

"You almost sound as if you believe in the Loch Ness Monster!" he exclaimed in disbelief,

Mr. MacDougal turned to stare at him.

"Well, now, we have a saying in Scotland, ye ken, and it goes something like this: 'Seeing is believing.'"

"You mean you *have* seen it? But I thought you said..." the man gabbled.

"I didn't *say* I *hadna* seen it. I just said I hadn't seen it when I had a boat full of people."

Fred gasped in surprise and nearly swallowed his pencil. His eyes began to sparkle like the sun as it reflected off the water.

"But when *did* you see it?" he breathed.

Mr. MacDougal looked thoughtful and his eyes took on a far away look.

"I'll tell you. It was late one afternoon. The sun was just thinking about setting. Mist was rising off the surface of the loch and it was very, very quiet." He dropped his voice to a whisper so that everyone had to lean forwards to catch what he was saying.

"It was turning chilly. Robbie and I were just clearing up the boat after a busy day's sailing. He was sweeping inside the cabin and I was scrubbing the deck."

He paused to look round at the spellbound faces of his passengers. "I heard it first," he said, raising his voice dramatically. "There was a kind of

64

rumbling noise in the bushes. I didna think much of it at the time – just a bird, or some holiday-makers messing about I thought. But then I smelled it! It was a very strange, strong smell, of earth and leaves and, I canna explain it – a sort of a smell of *age*."

Fred gulped. "Go on," he said and his voice came out in a squeak.

"And that was when I saw it! It came lumbering out of the undergrowth and dived straight into the water without a sideways glance. The water frothed and foamed like the contents of a witch's cauldron and as it swam away, it left behind a huge, wide, silvery wake."

Fred had noticed, as he stared at the loch, how everything, from the biggest speed boat to the smallest duck left a large trail of smooth water behind it as it moved. How big, he wondered, must Nessie be if she had left behind a *huge, wide* wake?

"And what...what did it look like?" he managed to ask.

"Yes, do tell us what it looked like," someone else called excitedly.

"You must remember that it was getting dark and it all happened very quickly," Mr. MacDougal whispered. "And it shocked me so much that I just stood there hardly daring to breathe. Anyway, I can tell ye this: it was far, far bigger than a double-decker bus, only black and kind of shiny, and it had more humps on its back than a fairground ride. Its neck was as long as a ladder, only sort of bendy, and it had a wee head on the end of it with flashing red eyes, like the lights on a level crossing when a train's coming. Its tail put me in mind of a kangaroo and the noise it made was that of a hungry pig with a chest infection. Its feet, nay, I couldna see its feet." Mr. MacDougal shook his head in disappointment. "But there was no doubt in my mind that I had seen the Loch Ness Monster and all the while I had goose pimples on my arms the size of Ben Nevis."

"And did your son see it too?" someone asked.

"Unfortunately he didn't. By the time I came to my senses and thought to call him, the creature had disappeared."

It went quiet for a while after that.

Granny, who had been asleep all this time, had slipped sideways and was leaning heavily against the man on her left, a total stranger. Her glasses had slipped down her nose and she was snoring softly.

Fred wasn't sure what to do. He smiled at the man uncertainly and was about to nudge Granny awake when, thankfully, she gave a loud grunt and woke herself up.

"Did someone mention ice cream?" she asked, sitting upright, and wiping a spot of dribble from the sleeve of the stranger's coat.

Someone sniggered, but Fred had other things on his mind. He was nervously fingering the piece of grey and green material, which he had been keeping in his pocket.

"I found this earlier on," he whispered timidly. "Or rather, my dog did. I wonder, do you think the Loch Ness Monster, the one you saw, could have caught itself on a bush and left this behind?"

Mr. MacDougal glanced at the scrap of fabric and his eyes sparkled for an instant, but then he shook his head.

"Good heavens, no laddie. When I saw the Monster, the *real, genuine* Monster that is, it was a very long time ago."

"When did you see it?" Fred asked impatiently. "Last week? Last year?"

"Och no! We're talking about fifteen years ago."

# Chapter 16

Granny thanked Mr. MacDougal for a lovely boat trip, even though she had slept through most of it. Then she and Fred went to sit on one of the wooden benches that were dotted about by the side of the loch.

Fred's head was buzzing with bits of information. He tried to explain it to Granny, but it all came out a bit garbled and mixed up. He seemed to be telling her something about a girl called Mary Rose and a giant newt.

"Well I never!" she exclaimed every few seconds. "That's something to tell your dad."

"Better not," Fred said promptly. "You remember what he said to me? I'm not to mention it again. But I can tell you can't I Granny?"

They sat for a while, enjoying the warm sunshine. Fred, who was busily trying to write up his notes, translate what he'd written into English and decode his spellings, had tied Monty to one of the legs of the bench they were sitting on. This proved to be a satisfactory arrangement at first, while the dog was dozing. However, when he woke up, every time a stray Canada goose or a swan came dangerously near, careless of its own safety, he would suddenly launch himself at it, dragging the bench with him.

"How am I supposed to write when you keep jogging me?" Fred moaned at the dog, looking up for an instant and realising that they were now only a few centimetres from the loch. They were so near, in fact, that Granny's feet were dangling in the water.

"I fancy a nice cup of tea in the hotel," she said, wriggling her toes and smacking her lips. "How about you, Fred?"

"Well, I *would* like to talk to some of the guests again," he replied. "I need some more information for my notebook. But I thought you said it was too expensive."

"And so it was. But don't you worry your head about money. I've been saving my spare change in a jar all year, ready for this holiday."

Fred shouldn't really have been surprised. After all, he had seen his Granny pay the bill in the hotel, yesterday, with a bag full of five pence pieces.

While he untangled Monty from the bench and put on the jumper he wore when he played cricket, Granny tugged on her trainers, wriggled into her white track suit top and pushed a stray strand of grey hair behind her ear.

There was a large white van parked outside the hotel today. It had the letters 'THE CLANSMAN

HOTEL' written in bold red letters across its side. There was other writing on it too:

"SEE MONSTER VIEWS FROM OUR BEAUTIFUL BOATS

AND MAMMOTH SCENERY FROM OUR COMFORTABLE COFFEE LOUNGE," Fred read out loud. "I don't think the people I spoke to saw Nessie when they were in a boat did they? I think they said they were sitting in the lounge," he added.

"I don't think they mean Nessie when they say 'MONSTER VIEWS.' It's what they call a play on words. That ice cream you just had was a monster one."

"You sound just like my dad," Fred laughed cheekily, tying Monty's lead to the railings.

This time Fred entered the hotel through the same door as Granny. It opened when they were only half way up the steps.

"Oh it's you two again," the man called Fergal hissed rudely through the side of his mouth. "I'd ask you why you don't just come and stay here, except we're full."

"The ravens would have to leave the Tower before I'd stay here, young man!" Granny snapped.

"Er, you what?" Fergal replied dumbly.

"There's a saying that if the ravens ever leave the Tower of London..." Fred started to explain.

"*Now* who's sounding like your dad?" Granny said. Then she turned to Fergal. "Don't bother to show us to the lounge, sonny. We know the way."

"All right, but don't go annoying the guests again with your stupid questions," he called after them. Fred gave the man his rudest stare and Fergal stared right back at him and then stuck his tongue out.

"Is Fergal looking after you?" a voice called from the reception desk. It was Mr. MacNoodle. "May I say how nice it is to see you here again today?"

"Why, thank you very much. And may I say how nice it is for us to be here," Granny said, speaking as if she had a mouth full of marbles. "Your – er- *doorman* says the hotel is full. That must make you feel very happy with money being as tight as it is at the moment."

"Aye, that it does. But we've had our ups and downs, I don't mind telling you. Up until a few years ago the hotel was only about a quarter full every week and we were in danger of going out of business."

"Then what happened?" Granny interrupted.

"A miracle, that's what. The Loch Ness Monster put in an appearance and the hotel's been full ever since."

"What a stroke of luck!" Granny remarked.

"Shall I show you through to the lounge?" Mr. MacNoodle offered, changing the subject suddenly. "And would you like to see a menu, or perhaps you'd like some tea?"

"Thank you very much," Granny replied, darting a withering look at the doorman. "But we've had luncheon already."

What they'd actually had were some fish paste sandwiches left over from yesterday's journey; some salt and vinegar crisps and half a bar of Turkish Delight each. "I'd like a coke for Fred here, please, and a pot of hot water for me. I've brought my own tea bag."

"Certainly, madam," the hotel manager said, and escorted them into the lounge.

# Chapter 17

Fred and Granny stayed in the hotel far longer than they had intended. Granny had played a few hands of cards with some of the residents whilst Fred had 'interviewed' those who had seen the Loch Ness Monster and seemed only too keen to talk about it.

"I hope he's not bothering you!" Granny shouted across the room at one point, remembering what that rude man, Fergal, had said.

"Oh no, not at all," had come the prompt reply. "What a charming young boy he is – so polite and so good at listening. We'd be delighted to answer his questions any time."

Fred was feeling very happy with himself. He'd been complimented on his behaviour; he'd learned a lot of valuable information and some of the guests had insisted on buying him drinks and an ice cream. Granny had feasted, too, on the little cakes that had been provided for the other visitors with their tea and coffee.

It was as they were leaving that Granny decided she would need to pay a visit to the 'little girls' room' before they headed back to the campsite. One of the waitresses kindly pointed her in the right direction. Fred hung about in the entrance hall, trying to avoid the snooty glare of the horrible Fergal.

"May I ask how long you'll be staying here?" a voice suddenly asked, making Fred jump. It was Mr. MacNoodle.

"Until Saturday. We've got a week," he replied.

"Well we look forward to welcoming you here at the Clansman Hotel whenever you feel like it. I must say the guests have all told me how much they like talking to you. Perhaps the next time you come you'd like to sample one of our speciality ice creams? On the house of course," he added.

Fred beamed with pleasure. "Spectacular!" was all he could find to say, followed a little later by an embarrassed, "Thank you," as he remembered his manners.

He couldn't wait to tell Granny. Hey - that was a thought – where was she?

He was just beginning to wonder if he should go and look for her, when he saw her nose flattened against the glass of the front doors. He raced to join her before Fergal could beat him to it and offer one of his snide remarks, only, for once, there didn't seem to be any sign of him. Fred had to open the door all by himself.

"Where have you been?" he asked Granny impatiently. "I thought you'd got lost."

"I came out of one of the doors at the back," she replied, chuckling to herself and winking at him. "I got lost. Come on, untie the dog. I've got something to show you."

Fred couldn't think what there could possibly be to interest him at the back of the hotel, but he did as he was told and followed her.

They walked along the front of the building and then turned left by a clump of bushes, following a path that Fred hadn't noticed until this minute. Monty had suddenly turned into his 'super-tracker-dog mode' and was nearly pulling his arm out of its socket.

Next they jogged the width of the building and then turned right along another little gravel path that was very overgrown with nettles and ivy. Fred rounded a sharp corner and then came to an abrupt standstill as Monty attacked a tall fence with his nose. Granny, coming round the bend a few seconds later, very nearly cannoned into them, but Fred was too busy staring at the fence to notice. It was covered in signs with the word 'DANGER!' scrawled all over them and everywhere there were crudely drawn pictures of skulls and crossbones and live wires. Someone had painted the words 'KEEP OUT' lots of times in thick red paint, straight on to the fence.

"Is this it?" Fred asked feeling disappointed. "Is this all you wanted to show me? Only I think we're on private land and I don't think we should be here."

"No, it isn't actually," Granny said, sounding a bit put out. "But someone's gone a bit mad with the signs, don't you think? One would have been enough. I had a look through the gaps in the fence and all I could see was a mouldy old wooden shed that looks as if it might fall down at any minute. Who'd want to go in there anyway?"

"What are we doing here then?" Fred insisted. Monty had begun to bark frantically and was pulling on his lead so hard that he was nearly choking. Now he was Monty the vacuum cleaner. His big, black, rubbery nose had gone into overtime in the sniffing department once again, and he was in danger of hoovering a few pine cones up his nostrils - and half the path. Fred had no choice but to follow him.

Granny found herself having to run to keep up with them and by the time Monty finally stopped, she was very out of breath.

"This is what I thought you'd like to see!" she exclaimed, pointing at the magnificent view. "Look how peaceful it is here, Fred. It's just right for a spot of fishing, away from the crowds."

But Fred wasn't listening. He had gone very quiet, and when Granny turned to look at him, she noticed how pale he was. He was staring down at his feet, looking at a strange print in the damp soil.

"What is it dear?" she asked, taking off her glasses and wiping them on her track suit top. "I can't make it out."

"It's ... the print ... of a ... flipper," he said very quietly. "And look," he added, examining the earth all round them, "there's another!"

As they stood there, trying to make sense of the marks in the mud, the bushes seemed to crowd in on them. Where the sunlight filtered through the trees, the leaves were a brilliant lime green, as though someone had taken a highlighter pen to them. But where the sun couldn't reach, the shadows were darker than ever. It was like trying to see through a brick wall. There was a damp, sour smell oozing up from the ground and Fred screwed up his nose in disgust.

"What do you think made those marks, Granny?" he asked, after a while.

"A frogman?" Granny suggested. And then, seeing the disappointed look on her grandson's face, she said, "Well don't ask me. How am I supposed to know? But people do swim underwater here, looking for monsters, don't they?"

Fred had assumed that the marks were made by something altogether different and began to feel rather stupid. For once, he decided to keep his thoughts to himself.

Monty had been sitting patiently for a whole minute, his tongue lolling from the side of his mouth, looking at the two of them questioningly, but all at once he was off, plunging into the bushes, almost pulling Fred off his feet.

This time Fred let go of the lead. No way was he going to chase after him. He told himself that it was because of the thick barrier of nettles that barred his way, but he knew it wasn't. There was something else stopping him. And there was more than a load of nettles and one mad dog in there, he was sure of it.

"Don't worry," Granny said to him, breaking the silence. "He'll come back to us when he's ready."

"Let's go," Fred said. "We'll wait for him back at the shed. I don't like it here."

Granny nodded and she was just turning to retrace her steps along the path, when she spotted something sticking out from behind a hawthorn bush.

"Why, it's a bike, Fred! What's it doing here, I wonder?"

"It looks like it's got a trailer stuck on the back of it and it's got writing on it," Fred said, helping her to drag it out of the undergrowth. "Look! SEE MONSTER VIEWS FROM OUR..." he began. "It's got the same writing on it as the van we saw outside the hotel. It must belong to Mr. MacNoodle. But what's it doing here?"

"Somebody must have borrowed it and couldn't be bothered to return it. Come on; let's put it back where it belongs. It's all right. We don't have to go back inside the hotel," Granny said. "We'll just prop it up on the railings next to the van."

Just then, a loud howling sound reached them, followed a fraction later by a dog that came so fast he was like a bullet. His tail was tucked firmly between his legs and when Fred reached out to catch him, he could feel him shaking like a pneumatic drill.

# Chapter 18

By the time Fred and Granny were nearly at the campsite, Monty was almost back to his normal self, although he did stay very close to Fred's side, which was most unusual for him.

"What do you suppose frightened him like that?" Fred called as he waited for Granny to catch up.

"Search me," she replied. "I have no way of knowing what goes on in that dog's brain, or if he even has one."

"I didn't like it much by those bushes either. It felt all spooky and weird."

"The trouble with you, Fred Boggitt, is that you've got too much imagination. You take after your Grandpa Boggitt. It's all that telly you watch."

Fred didn't bother to reply.

"What do you think was in the shed then?" he asked instead.

Granny stopped to look at the view while she caught her breath. The sun had dipped behind a large black cloud and it had turned much colder.

"I should think it's the hotel's generator. You know, the thing that makes their electricity, if there's a power cut. They have to have signs warning people these days, in case someone hurts themselves and decides to sue the hotel for a lot of money."

They had reached the campsite now, and Monty had decided that it was time to take off on his own again and jump all over Mr. Boggitt, who was waving to them from the top of the hill. Next to him were two, small, dark green tents.

"Your new home!" he yelled to them across the field. "What do you think?"

Fred ran the rest of the way. "They look great, Dad, but why have you put flags all over the hedge?"

"So you can find your way home of course," Mr. Boggitt explained, looking pleased with himself. "The flags will help you to see which tents are ours."

Fred secretly thought that he would have known which tents were theirs without the flags. For one thing, the Boggitts were still the only campers on this side of the field and, for another, the remains of the blackened tree that stood next to where the new stove had been, was itself quite a landmark.

"Right," was all he said, but then another thought struck him. He now noticed a pile of stones and some large logs, arranged in a square on the ground. There was a cloud of black smoke coming from the middle of a few sorry-looking sticks in the centre of the square.

"Dad? Where's the new stove gone?" he asked.

"He's packed it away, along with loads of other things," Mrs. Boggitt said. Fred wondered why he could only see part of his mother's face, her mouth in fact, as she spoke through a tiny hole at the top of the tent flap. Why didn't she pull the zip down? "He ran out of gas," the mouth continued, "and he couldn't get a refill. Besides, there isn't much room now we've had to downsize."

"Come and sit down, Granny," Mr. Boggitt said quickly, pointing to one of the chairs. "You look a bit tired. Had a good day?"

"Yes we have, thank you," Granny said, before Fred could say anything and get told off for talking 'Monster talk.'

"Well, just let me get this fire going and you can tell us all about it. Fred, help me get some more wood will you? There's nothing like cooking on a real fire and tonight we're going to celebrate with a slap up meal."

Just at that moment a face appeared on the other side of the hedge.

"Oh hello," Mervyn said. "I was just collecting some wood myself. Oh! New tents, I see. And you've bought nylon this time. Good idea. They're so much lighter to carry and so much easier to put up, don't you think? Um, you did check the zips to test that they're the non-rusting kind didn't..."

It was then he caught sight of Mrs. Boggitt's eyes squinting at him through the little hole in the tent flap.

"Oh dear! You didn't did you? Well never mind, a bit of soap should do the trick. And if I might make another little suggestion," he added, before anyone could stop him. "If you look for dead branches up in the trees, instead of using damp ones from the ground, you won't get all that nasty black smoke."

"Come on son," Mr. Boggitt said through clenched teeth, leading Fred away by his arm and glaring at his neighbour over his shoulder, "let's get some wood. We'll soon have a good blaze going. Goodbye Melvyn."

"Hurry up then," Granny coughed, covering her eyes with her hankie to stop the smoke from stinging them. "I'm dying for a nice cup of tea."

Mr. Boggitt and Fred hurried off and they had soon collected a carrier bag full of pine cones and some fairly dry tree bark and pine needles.

Mr. Boggitt held one of the pine cones in his hand and examined it.

"Do you know how you can tell that it's going to be a damp day, son?" he asked.

Fred thought for a moment, wondering if this was a trick question. "When water starts falling from the sky?" he replied.

"No, no Fred. When the pine cones close up. You see they shut tight to protect their seeds from the rain, as this one has done. And when I see them all closed up like this I think to myself, 'It must be a damp day today.' Honestly, you need to learn these things, son, you really do."

Fred nodded thoughtfully and began to sprint back up the hill.

He was surprised to see that his mum had finally emerged from her tent and that she and Granny had managed to get the fire going. It was burning merrily with a clear bright flame.

Mr. Boggitt's face was bright red by the time he reached the top of the field and he was quite out of breath. He threw his bag of pine cones down on the ground.

"We don't need those," Granny said irritatingly. "Mervyn gave us a whole sack full of dry branches, all cut up and ready to use. And I don't know why you had to put our tents at the top of this hill. It's like climbing Mount Kilimanjaro."

"*Because my copy of the 'Campers' Bible' says that high ground is good*," Mr. Boggitt snapped. "*Low ground soaks up water like a sponge, that's why! And you don't want to find yourself swimming in your tent when it rains do you?*"

"All right, keep your hair on! I only asked," Granny replied sulkily.

"Now Mother, what are we going to cook? Remember I promised everyone a slap-up meal," Mr. Boggitt said, with forced cheerfulness.

Mrs. Boggitt ducked her head back inside the tent and rummaged around. She picked up a couple of tins.

"Er, baked beans or spaghetti hoops," she shouted.

84

"Righty-ho! We'll eat it off our best china plates. Everything always tastes better off china plates. And look Fred. I've constructed this little gadget for resting bread on so that you can toast it. I made it out of a wire coat hanger. You put your slice of bread on this little shelf, like so, and then you hold it over the fire... Oh bother!"

"That's a whole loaf you've got through trying out that darned thing!" Granny complained. "Why don't you just *throw* the next one straight on the fire, it'll be quicker!"

# Chapter 19

When they eventually got round to eating their tea, the Boggitts were pleasantly surprised at how good it tasted.

The conversation was surprisingly relaxed too, as they sat round the camp fire telling each other about the events of the day.

"The only thing is," Mrs. Boggitt said, "Enid, the lady who helps Auntie Ethel and Uncle Walter out with the guest house, has had a nasty fall and broken her ankle. So your dad and I promised we'd help out tomorrow and..."

"That's all right mum," Fred said, looking at his watch.

"Granny and I have things to do, here, tomorrow. Now do you mind if I go to bed? Only I'm really, really tired." And just to prove it, he gave the most enormous yawn.

"Yes, all right, Poppet," Mrs. Boggitt said, feeling extremely surprised. Fred never, *ever*, volunteered to have an early night. "But I told Auntie..."

"Let the boy get to bed if he's tired, Mother. What you have to say will keep 'til morning," Mr. Boggitt said. "Goodnight, sleep tight, son. Don't let the bed bugs bite. And don't forget to brush your teeth."

Monty was surprised to be having an early night too, but realising that he'd had all the food he was going to get, he dashed to the tent and pushed in front of Fred to be first in.

It was a bit of a squash, but once they were both settled, it felt quite cosy. The dog scratched himself silly then tried rolling around for a bit, but when he found himself bouncing off the tent walls, he soon grew tired and slipped into sleep mode. Meanwhile, Fred tucked his feet into his sleeping bag, fished out his wind-up torch and his notebook, and began to read what he'd written over the past two days.

When Granny entered the tent with her hot water bottle and her mug of Horlicks, some three hours later, he was fast asleep. She got ready for bed, shoved Monty off her sleeping bag and squeezed herself inside.

Happily, it was a much better night for everyone. It was quiet - apart, that is, from the whining of a pesky mosquito which invited itself into Fred's tent in the middle of the night. Granny did her best to silence it by taking swipes at it with her tennis racket. This didn't actually do anything whatsoever to disturb the mosquito, but it did wear Granny out, so that she slept soundly for the rest of the night. That is, apart from the few times that she went to turn over and found herself rolling on top of Fred and squashing him.

Fred was the first to wake in the morning.

"Granny, are you awake?" he whispered. He could tell she was because her face was only one centimetre away from his and her eyes were open.

"No," she said, squinting at him over the edge of her sleeping bag.

"Only my alarm's going to go off in one minute and I don't want it to give you a heart attack."

"Switch it off then dear."

Fred leaned over and flicked off the switch and then sat up. Something inside his sleeping bag was digging into him and he realised it was his notebook and torch. He realised annoyingly that he'd gone to sleep and left his torch switched on. That would cost him another half hour of his life winding it up. Never mind, before too long he'd have muscles like Tarzan.

"I've been going through my notes and I've noticed something very strange. Just listen to this will you," he said urgently and began to read from his little book.

"SIGHTINGS OF THE LOCH NESS MONSTER AS RECORDED BY FRED BOGGITT." He cleared his throat.

"Mary Smith, Wednesday October 5th, 1885. 'It was the biggest thing I ever saw, with a neck like a horse.'

"Salmon angler, Saturday July 10th, 1895. 'It had a hump like an upturned boat.'

"The Reverend Peter Booth, Tuesday January 27th, 1933. 'It moved in a circle and had an 8 foot hump.'

"Morris Johnson, Thursday …"

"Fred, don't think for a minute that I'm not interested, but it'll be Christmas soon," Granny groaned.

"No, no. It's going to get interesting soon, I promise. I'm getting to the good bit," Fred said, and carried on reading.

"Helen Shortcake, Sunday 30th November, 1999. 'It dived into the loch. It was the size of a cart horse. Its mouth was opening and closing.'

"Monday, April 12th, 2007. Amanda Addlington. 'It sailed across the loch as I sat watching. I couldn't believe my eyes.'

"Sunday, April 18th, 2007. Mrs. K. Tiffany. 'I got a good look at it as it swam to and fro. It had at least four humps.'

"Monday, April 26th, 2007. Bertie Bourne. 'I was waiting to have my tea and suddenly there it was. It had a single triangular hump.'

"And now I'm skipping on," Fred said speaking quickly now. He pretended not to notice Granny cheering as he turned over quite a few pages. "Sunday, 1st February, 2009. Betty Blight. 'I was reading the paper. I looked up and there it was, zigzagging across the water.'

"Monday, 9th February, 2009. Sally Harris. 'I just happened to look out of the window and I saw this mighty creature sailing across the water. My heart nearly stopped beating.'

"Mr. Gordon Campbell. 'We all saw her just the other day. It was on Monday actually, the twelfth of April. It was after tea and we were all lined up, sipping a spot of sherry...'"

"Just a minute!" Granny said, sitting bolt upright. She had stopped pulling faces and was looking quite excited. "I was there! I remember him saying it – those very words."

"All those reports of sightings, all months or even years apart and then suddenly you get to two thousand and seven and there's one *practickly* every week. And I only read you a few of them. There are *loads* more."

"Yes, yes. I'll take your word for that," Granny said quickly. "Do you know Fred, I thought at the time that it was a very strange thing to say. I mean, the settees and chairs were arranged in little groups on the two occasions that we've been in the lounge. Why would Mr. Campbell say that they were 'all lined up'? It's almost as if they were waiting for something to happen."

Fred lay back with his hands behind his head, and Monty, sensing the excitement in the atmosphere, roused himself and began licking Fred's face with his hot, sticky tongue.

"That's exactly what I was thinking," Fred said, pushing the dog away. "And have you noticed that the sightings I've written down all happened on either a Sunday or Monday?"

Granny nodded thoughtfully.

"I'd say it's a very strange Monster indeed that puts in appearances as regularly as episodes of Coronation Street. And, do you know, dear, there are some other things that have been bothering me too. For instance, I'd like to know..."

"Get up, get up, sleepy heads!" Mr. Boggitt sang as he poked his head through the tent flap. "We've had our showers and by the time you've had yours, breakfast will be well and truly ready."

Granny waited until he was out of earshot before she spoke.

"As soon as they set off to Auntie Ethel's, we'll go and do a bit of exploring. Do you realise it was Sunday yesterday? I wonder if our 'Monster' put in an appearance. If we get to the hotel early we might get a chance to look at the seating arrangements."

"Good idea. And I want to find out what it was that frightened Monty in the bushes. I think I was a bit of a wimp, running away like that, so I'm going to make myself go into those bushes and have a good look round. It's called *conkering* your fears. And Monty can conker his at the same time too."

# Chapter 20

It was a sunny, fairly warm morning. For once, everyone agreed that Mr. Boggitt had got it right. There is nothing quite like cooking on an open fire and eating breakfast outside. And Monty wasn't the only one who was sent wild by the smell of bacon sizzling. The scrambled eggs were cooked just right – not burned to the bottom of the pan as they had been the day before. And Fred had finally mastered the art of his dad's 'do-it-yourself-toaster'.

They had finished eating, done the washing up and cleared away when Mr. Boggitt began his usual hunt for his car keys. Mrs. Boggitt had bought him a little gadget to help him find them, because he was *always* losing them. If you whistled loudly, the keys would whistle back – or at least that was the idea. But the keys whistled back whenever they felt like it; if a car or lorry passed by the house; or if anyone breathed. It had driven them all mad, so eventually they had put the gadget out with the rubbish. Mrs. Boggitt said they were probably still whistling in a landfill site somewhere on the other side of the world.

"Aha!" he shouted triumphantly after a while, waving his keys about in the air. "The Boggitt taxi leaves in ten minutes."

"Give Ethel my love," Granny called, winking at Fred.

"You can give it to her yourself," Mrs. Boggitt replied.

Granny looked surprised. "But not today. She won't mind if she doesn't see me today."

"No I'm sure she won't," Mrs. Boggitt said shortly, putting on her lipstick and fluffing up her hair. "But I promised her we'd take Fred to see her."

"Aw, mum," Fred complained. "Granny and I've got urgent business..."

"Well, it'll have to wait 'til we get back, won't it?"

"The lad's coming with us Mother," Mr. Boggitt said sternly. "I've told him before. He has a duty to his family. Family are more important than..."

"Don't start, Fred senior. I've already got a headache. He knows he's got to come don't you Poppet? It was nice Auntie Ethel who knitted that outfit for your Action Man at Christmas, remember?"

"Action Men don't wear pink," Fred muttered.

"I know, darling, but she had the wool left over from her god-daughter's baby."

"Did she knit that too?" Fred said cheekily, but he knew when he was beaten.

Granny heaved a sigh and went to find her best hat. Monty had been sitting on it and it took her several minutes to push it back into shape and even then it looked very squashed, but nobody said anything.

"I hope you've washed behind your ears, Fred," Mr. Boggitt said playfully. "Your Auntie Ethel's sure to look."

# Chapter 21

A s it happened, the trip to Inverness wasn't nearly as bad as Fred had thought it would be.

Auntie Ethel and Uncle Walter's guest house was on a busy street on the outskirts of Inverness. It was a very narrow building, but Fred counted the windows and worked out that it had four storeys.

The sat. nav. managed to find it on the fourth attempt and the Boggitts piled out of the car.

"Auntie Ethel," Fred asked when she had finished hugging and kissing him and telling him how much he had grown, "why is your house called 'Loch Glimpse'? I mean all you can see from your windows are loads and loads of houses."

Mrs. Boggitt gasped. "Fred, don't be so rude. It's none of your business if Auntie Ethel wants to call her guest house a silly name."

"Oh, don't you worry dear," his auntie said, presenting him with yet another outfit for his

Action Man - bright yellow this time. "You're not the first to ask and you won't be the last. You see dear, we couldn't afford anything nearer to the loch than this because property there is so expensive, but the man who fixed our satellite dish said that you can glimpse the loch if you stand on the roof."

Fred was about to ask if she'd been up to find out for herself, when Granny interrupted him.

"You've done the lounge out nicely, Ethel. I like the tartan wallpaper and the portraits of the MacBoggitts on the wall. And it's quite nice having bagpipes playing on the gramophone, even though it is switched up too loud."

Auntie Ethel smiled proudly. "You haven't seen anything yet. You wait until you see the rest of the house," she said smiling broadly and winking at them.

They all got to see the rest of the house fairly soon after that. Because of Enid's broken ankle, Auntie Ethel was short staffed, so she set the Boggitt's off, Granny included, cleaning out the rooms on the ground floor. After that, Mr. and Mrs. Boggitt helped to prepare the lunch, while Fred and Granny cleaned upstairs.

Next, Fred helped Granny to make the beds. Afterwards they scrubbed a few washbasins – those that didn't have false teeth soaking in them, or dirty nappies - and then Fred hung on to Granny's dangling legs while she sat on the window sill and cleaned the outside of the attic windows.

96

"Well Fred, I do believe I can see the loch, just as Auntie Ethel said. Either that or it's someone's garden pond. It's hard to tell when it's glinting in the sun."

"When do you suppose we can go back to the campsite? Only I've had enough of all this housework," Fred moaned as he wiped off some 'Windowshine' he'd accidentally spilled on a white blouse that was hanging over the back of a chair.

"Now, now, it doesn't hurt to lend a helping hand now and again. You remember that!" Granny said primly. Then, "Soon I hope," she added.

By this time lunch was ready so Fred was volunteered into serving the guests' food, whilst the rest of the Boggitts washed up, cleaned up and started to get tea ready.

By the middle of the afternoon, Fred and Granny were finally told by Mr. and Mrs. Boggitt that they could return to the campsite on the bus, taking Monty with them. They would return later, they said, after tea had been cleared away.

Fred was pleased to be going, but he was also feeling surprisingly contented.

"I got five pounds from Auntie Ethel because she hadn't had time to buy me an Easter egg; then there's the pocket money you gave me, Dad, *and* ten of the guests staying at Auntie Ethel's gave me a pound each," he explained cheerfully, as he stood on the doorstep saying his goodbyes.

"The guests said what a lovely young man you are and how they loved hearing your Monster stories," Auntie Ethel said, giving him yet another kiss.

On hearing the word 'Monster' Mr. Boggitt looked extremely irritated. He opened his mouth to give his son a telling off, when one of the elderly residents called out from somewhere behind them,

"You must be very proud of your son sir. And I think I can see where he gets his good looks and charm from."

This brought a modest smile to Mr. Boggitt's face and Granny said quickly, "Come on Fred. It's time we were on our way."

# Chapter 22

Once back at the campsite, Fred ran to their tent to take off his tie and fetch his carry case with his binoculars and all his other gadgets. Granny waited for him near the path that would take them down to the loch.

By the time Fred rejoined her, she was messing about with a piece of wood, bending it over her knee.

"What are you *doing?*" he asked breathlessly.

"Oh, just making a little bow and some arrows out of these bits of hazel," she replied, fishing a penknife and some string out of her handbag.

"I forgot you go to archery lessons now, don't you?"

"Oh, I used to shoot years ago, long before you were born. Got my 'Backwoodsman' badge. I had to survive for a *whole week* in the wilderness."

"Spectacular! Wow! That bow looks well neat. Will you make me one?"

Granny picked up some feathers that were scattered on the ground and began sticking them to the arrows with sticky black tape.

"You can have a go with this one first. See how you get on. But first, if you'd care to go and stand over there with a pine cone on your head, I'll show you what a good shot I am," she said, pointing to the broad trunk of an old oak tree.

"Um, I don't think I will if you don't mind. I kind of need my head today."

"It's strange how it's all coming back to me. Honestly Fred, my instructor says I've made real progress over the past few weeks. I've even been known to hit the target five times out of ten *and* I got a bull's eye once. "

Fred laughed and began running down the path with Monty in hot pursuit. The dog hadn't liked being tied up in Auntie Ethel's back yard one bit and had howled all morning. Of course, no one could hear him because of the bagpipes, but he wasn't to know that. It was a rule that no dogs were allowed in the house, so that was that.

Half way down the path, Fred stopped and waited. Granny had slung her bow over her shoulder and fastened the arrows to her handbag with a piece of string.

"You look very thoughtful dear," she said as she caught up with him.

"It's my brain. It won't stop thinking things. All the time when I was doing that cleaning for Auntie Ethel, I couldn't switch it off. It was driving me mad. Like when I've got a hard sum at school and it won't let itself be worked out."

"Give me an example."

"Well, there was this one about a picture frame and I had to work out the area..."

"No Fred, not the sum! I meant tell me what your brain's been thinking about this morning."

"Well, like yesterday, on the boat. Why did Mr. MacDougal say he'd seen the *real, genuine* Monster? What other kind is there? And why are those doormen so nasty to us and why..."

"My, you have been busy, haven't you?" Granny laughed. "I tell you what, let's have a cup of tea and then we'll talk about it. I'm a bit hot and tired to be honest."

"I'll be able to treat you today. Now I've got all this money, I'm rich!"

"You hang on to it, dear. I've got a tea bag and I'm sure I can afford to treat you to a drink," Granny said, patting her handbag.

By this time they had reached the hotel. Fred was surprised to see that the front doors were wide open and they hadn't even started up the steps. He shrugged his shoulders, hitched Monty to the railings, and followed Granny up past the stone lions.

There was no sign of either of the doormen, and Fred couldn't help feeling relieved. Mr. MacNoodle was standing at the reception desk and he smiled when he saw the two of them coming across the carpet towards him.

Granny handed him the bow she had made and asked him if he would look after it. He gave her a very strange look, but hung it on a hook behind him.

"No doormen today?" she said.

"Och no. It's their day off. Yesterday they had the afternoon and evening off, but don't worry, they'll be in this evening at 6 o'clock to serve the guests their dinner. Now will it be the lounge and a drink you're wanting? And I haven't forgotten your ice cream young man."

Fred was rather full because he'd eaten a large meal at Auntie Ethel's – stuff the guests hadn't wanted – but he wasn't about to say so. Instead he smiled and followed Mr. MacNoodle into the lounge.

The visitors were eating sandwiches and cakes, handed to them by the smiling waitress they had seen before.

"I see the guests are sitting in a line today," Granny said matter-of-factly as she squeezed in beside Mr. Campbell and helped herself to a salmon and cucumber sandwich. She *hadn't* had any lunch as she hadn't fancied the fatty lamb and frozen sprouts that were on offer at her sister's.

"Yes indeed," Mr. MacNoodle replied, signalling to the waitress to fetch Fred's ice cream. "Fergal and Hamish like to re-arrange the furniture on a Sunday morning, before they go off. They say it makes a nice change for the guests to sit in a line, so that they can make the most of the view."

"I bet they do," Granny said before she could stop herself.

"Just think," Morag called across the room, "if we hadn't been sitting like that we might have missed seeing the Monster altogether."

"Has anybody here ever managed to get a photo of it?" Granny asked innocently.

"No, no, they haven't unfortunately," Mr. Campbell said, looking around him for confirmation. "It's something to do with the glass in the window, I think. The light bounces off it too much. I'm no expert though you understand."

"A newspaper reporter stayed here for a whole week once, when we told him we'd seen the Monster," Brenda said. "He didn't manage to get a photo either."

"That's because *no one* saw the Monster that week, Brenda. I know, I was here the first week in November," Morag explained.

"I bet they didn't," Granny muttered.

"Sorry, what did you say?"

"Did you see it yesterday by any chance?" Granny asked instead, "because it was Sunday yesterday."

"I know fine what day it was," Morag replied irritably. "I don't need you telling me. And no, we didn't see it. I'd have told you if we had."

"Never mind. Better luck tonight maybe?" Granny said, winking at Mr. MacNoodle.

The hotel owner looked rather hot and bothered and he leant down to whisper in Granny's ear. "We never know when the thing is going to appear. It's very unfortunate. People come and stay here hoping to catch sight of it and when it doesn't materialize they get very disappointed. Why, some of them even demand their money back."

"But when it *does* come, you *are* certain that it's the real thing are you?" Granny asked innocently and perhaps just a fraction too loudly.

"Why, Madam, whatever are you suggesting?" Mr. MacNoddle spluttered.

"Of course it's the real thing," the woman called Brenda shouted. "What are you trying to say?"

"What's that? What's she saying?" someone else demanded.

"She thinks we don't know the Loch Ness Monster when we see it!" someone else explained.

"Rubbish! The woman doesn't know what she's talking about. Coming in here and eating our sandwiches!"

"And our shortbread biscuits."

"But I have my... my... hotel's reputation to think about," Mr. MacNoodle was stammering. "Why would you think that our Monster's a fake?"

"Calm down everybody!" Granny shouted. "It was just a simple question. Forget I spoke. I'm sorry," she said, turning to the manager. "You should know what the real Monster looks like. I didn't mean..."

"Well, I haven't actually *seen* it," he said, straightening his tie. "By the time they called me into the lounge, it had disappeared."

"This is delicious," Fred said into the silence that followed this remark. "Do you want to try a bit Granny?"

"No, no," she said quickly, staring at the ice cream, which was still as tall as the Eiffel Tower, even though he'd been tucking into it for the past ten minutes. "I think it's time we settled our bill and left."

"The hot water's on the house," Mr. MacNoodle explained and led the way hastily out of the lounge.

Granny retrieved her bow quickly and hurried out of the hotel, closely followed by Fred, who had had the good sense to bring his ice cream with him.

# Chapter 23

The sun had gone in by this time and the sky had turned a dismal grey colour. A stiff breeze was blowing from the loch too, churning the water.

Monty tugged so hard on his lead the minute he saw Fred that the railing came unstuck and trailed behind him as he bolted across the flowerbeds.

Once Granny had done her best rugby tackle on him and rescued the bit of railing, she and Fred set off along the path. A quick look round told them that there was no one about to see them as they turned left and followed the track to the wooden shed.

They stopped for a while, working out what to do next.

"Do you still want to go and examine the bushes where Monty was given his scare?" Granny said, looking closely at Fred. "Only it's beginning to get dark, even though it's still fairly early."

Fred nodded, biting his lip. "I've been waiting all day for this. I'm not chickening out now."

Monty, however, had other ideas. He was already digging his paws into the ground, making it clear that he wasn't prepared to go any further. Fred had no choice but to drag him.

"Come on!" he urged. "You're far too fat for me to carry." However, just then, such was the contradictory nature of this stubborn little canine, that he changed his mind and launched himself into the bushes instead.

Fred and Granny walked a little further along the path, debating whether to follow him or not. Fred didn't actually say anything, but he was feeling frightened - so much so that when some hazel catkins tickled his face and arms he nearly jumped out of his skin.

"Oh! Those things scared the life out of me!" he exclaimed, while Granny tried to reassure him.

"Do you think they'll ever let us back into the hotel after all that fuss about the Monster?" he asked eventually, trying to take his mind off his resolution to 'conker his fear', while they waited for Monty to reappear.

"I don't see why not. I only asked a simple question. But I'm not bothered. It's their loss. At least some of my other questions were answered."

"They *were* expecting the Monster last night weren't they?" Fred asked, cautiously pulling a few branches back and peering into the gloom – almost going into the bushes, but not quite. "That's why the chairs were all set out like that."

"Yes. And don't you think it's a *bit* of a coincidence that Hamish and Fergal just *happen* to have their days off on a Sunday and Monday?"

"I wonder if ...."

But Fred didn't get the chance to reveal what it was he was wondering, for at that moment he was interrupted by a series of explosive yapping sounds. These were followed by the sudden appearance of a hysterical dog, carrying in its mouth what looked like a dirty old trainer.

Granny recognised it at once.

"I know who *that* belongs to!" she exclaimed, wrestling it from Monty's mouth. It was the gaping hole in the toe and the grubby, chewed laces that did it. "The last time I saw that thing it was on Fergal's foot."

"Are you sure?" Fred asked. "But what's it doing here?"

"What do you mean, *am I sure*? Do dogs bark? Do lions roar? Is your dog stupid? Of course I'm sure! I just don't know what it's doing in the bushes."

Granny screwed her nose up in disgust and threw it back where it came from.

"Bother! What time is it?" Fred asked suddenly. "Do you think mum and dad will be back yet? Only I don't want to get into trouble." He peered at his watch. "Five o'clock!"

"Oh, they won't be back for ages. They'll have the washing up to do, and then they'll have to have a little natter with Ethel and Walter, and don't forget there's the drive back in the rush hour. Tell you what, let's have a look round and then we'll think of heading back."

But that wasn't *quite* how it turned out, for just as Fred and Granny plucked up the courage to go *into* the bushes to explore, they heard the distinct snorting and stamping of something that was quite definitely on its way *out*.

"What?" Fred said feeling thoroughly startled, looking round for Monty and spotting him sniffing the air and wagging his tail ecstatically.

"Shush!" Granny cautioned, holding a finger to her lips and pulling Fred down out of view. Then, "Aaah!" she yelped loudly.

"The Monster!" Fred exclaimed in terror.

"No – one of my arrows. I sat on it!"

She didn't say anything to her grandson, but she was feeling almost as nervous as he was.

The noises in the bushes ahead of them were growing louder and more menacing.

Fred looked at Granny, his eyes wide open and his mouth gaping. His heart was thumping so loudly he could hear it hammering in his ears. He hadn't been this frightened since Granny had been locked out of her maisonette and he'd got stuck in the cat-flap and his dad had threatened to force him out with a car-jack and a tub of margarine.

Monty, the born protector, took one look at Fred, gave a little grunt and headed off into the bushes again before anyone could stop him. And the very second he disappeared, a foul smell wafted from the undergrowth and Fred gasped in horror as the strangest creature he had ever set eyes on lumbered out of the brushwood. It was *big!* It was *huge! It was enormous!*

At least it was at the front. The Monster's head and neck *towered* over Fred as he sat on a tree stump rigid with fear, trying to stop himself from crying out.

Peering out from between his fingers, he saw its blood-red eyes flashing as the sun appeared for a second from behind a thick black cloud. He was trembling all over and his breath was coming in short gasps, but he steeled himself to look again, his curiosity getting the better of him.

Strangely, he could only see one fairly small bump where the creature's neck joined its body, not four humps as he had been led to believe. It had a long, thin, scaly tail too, just like some of the dinosaurs he'd seen in books and it thudded up and down on the ground as the beast waddled to the edge of the loch.

Fred felt for Granny's hand and held it tight. He could hear the creature creaking as it walked. It must be very, very old.

He could hardly believe what his eyes were telling him! He was *actually looking* at the Loch Ness Monster and on his first trip to Scotland too! Why, some people waited *years.*

Next to him, on the damp ground, he could feel Granny shaking too. He knew she was scared, but there was nothing he could do. If they made a run for it, there was no knowing how the creature would react, even though he hadn't read anything about it actually harming anyone.

Just as the Monster was about to dive into the loch, Fred noticed its feet. Even Mr. MacDougal, on his boat, hadn't seen the Monster's feet. And they were very unusual indeed. They were a bright pink colour. Fred gasped. They were *flippers*! So it *was* the Monster that had made the marks in the soil. He had been right after all.

And then, just when he thought he might die of excitement, the creature lunged into the water, opened its great mouth and bellowed!

"Aaaaaaaah! Och, Fergal mate, this water's blooming freezing."

"Will you stop moaning and get on with it. We're meant to be serving dinner at six," a voice at the rear of the animal replied.

"It's all right for you, but I've had one cold already this year – and will you stop treading on the back of my heels? I've got blisters from wearing these blessed flippers and they hurt like nobody's business."

"I like that! *I'm* the one who has to swim under water for half an hour."

"Och – stop exaggerating."

Fred jolted upright. He was thoroughly startled. Surely he hadn't just heard what he thought he'd heard? He turned to stare at Granny.

"Oh Fred," she whispered softly, shaking with laughter. "Your face is a picture! Don't tell me you really thought *that* was the Loch Ness Monster?"

Fred opened and closed his mouth like a sea trout, until at last he found his voice.

"No, um, no. Of course I didn't," he said indignantly, going very red in the face. "Stop looking at me like that! I *didn't* – not for a second. *Really!* We knew it was Fergal and Hamish. We said so didn't we?"

"All right, I believe you, but come on. We've got to hurry. They're about to sail past the lounge and give the residents a nice surprise. Let's go and watch – that is if Mr. MacNoodle will let us in!"

# Chapter 24

As luck would have it, there was no sign of Mr. MacNoodle as the two entered the hotel in a bit of a rush.

They were soon to discover that he was in the lounge trying to calm the residents, who, it appeared were still seething with anger over Granny's question about the Loch Ness Monster.

"Was it the real thing? I'll give her, 'was it the real thing?' if I ever clap eyes on her again," Morag was saying. "Who gives her the right...?"

"There, there, Morag, calm yourself," Mr. MacNoodle replied in his most soothing manner. "I can assure you that nobody in this hotel would *ever* be involved in anything as utterly dishonest as faking the legendary Monster. *It simply would not happen.* And now, I'm going to pour you another complimentary glass of sherry to soothe your nerves. Then, after dinner you can all watch football on our new, wide-screen telly. It's Celtic playing Rangers, so it should be a good match."

But it appeared the residents hadn't quite finished complaining yet.

"The cheek of the woman! As if I don't know the real Monster when I see it!" Brenda muttered, holding out her glass for a top up.

Mr. MacNoodle, realising that his sherry decanter had run dry, hurried to the bar for a refill.

"And that's the last time I squeeze up on the sofa to let her sit next to me, I can tell you."

Mr. Campbell had just finished speaking, when several things happened all at once. *Mrs.* Campbell spotted Granny hovering at the door with something that looked like a *bow* in her hand. Well - it was all too much for her to take in one afternoon! She stood up abruptly and pointed an angry finger in Granny's direction, at exactly the same moment that *Mr.* Campbell shot off the settee, where he had been sitting, and pointed a trembling digit in the direction of the loch.

"She's there!" Mrs. Campbell screeched, clutching her throat with her other hand.

"It's there!" Mr. Campbell screamed at the same time, his face turning as red as a fire engine.

And suddenly the place was in uproar.

As Mrs. Campbell had jumped from her chair, she had banged into the coffee table, sending two dishes of olives and Bombay Mix flying through the air.

As Mr. Campbell had catapulted from the settee, *he* had knocked over his sherry glass, sending a spray of sticky brown liquid all over Morag *and* the new lounge carpet.

Mr. MacNoodle, re-entering the room, pushed past Fred and Granny who were lurking by the door, uttered a scream of horror when he spotted the stain on his Axminster, fell on his hands and knees and began scrubbing at it with his tie.

"Quick, it's the Monster! Someone get a photograph before it vanishes in the weeds!" Brenda shrieked, running to the window and tripping over Mr. MacNoodle.

"Someone phone Ewan Yours at the Tartan Times," Morag yelled, trying to wipe the sherry off her dress with one of the table cloths, but not daring to take her eyes off the creature on the loch. "Tell him to get here quick."

"This is *so* exciting. This is the third time I've seen it and it just gets better and better," Mrs. Campbell trilled, forgetting all about Granny for the moment. "I can't wait to write my postcards."

"Is it really them?" Fred whispered, creeping into the room.

"Shush! Don't let them hear you. Yes it's Fergal and Hamish all right. They don't fool me."

It was strange, though. The sky had turned a plum colour and some of the sun's rays were managing to filter their way through the clouds, creating strange textures of light and dark on the surface of the water. A mist was rising too, so that it was hard to imagine that the strange shape making its unsteady progress past the lounge window was anything but the real, genuine Monster, in spite of the piece of material that had come loose and was flapping round its head.

For a moment, even Granny had felt a moment's uncertainty.

But as they watched, and the babble of excitement in the room grew louder and louder, the beast suddenly turned and began swimming jerkily back in the direction from which it had come.

"Quick, Fred," Granny whispered hoarsely, "they're heading back." She glanced at the clock on the wall. "It's twenty to six. They're serving dinner in twenty minutes. We've got to catch them red handed."

"But... but, shouldn't we tell someone? What can we do on our own?" Fred stammered, pulling back.

"You must be joking, dear. Who's going to believe us? Come *on*. If we don't go now we'll miss them."

# Chapter 25

They practically sprinted back to the bushes. Fred just had time to notice the bike with its trailer, half-hidden by the undergrowth, when the sound of splashing – and rather a lot of moaning and groaning – alerted them to the fact that the 'Monster' was returning! At least – half of it was.

Granny told Fred to crouch in the shadows where they wouldn't be seen. He was just doing as he was told, and listening to the sound of splashing drawing nearer and nearer, coming from somewhere to the right of them, when he became aware of another sound. Someone was approaching along the path to their left!

They were trapped! Unless they ran for cover in the bushes they were sure to be seen. Fred was scared that any movement they made would reveal their presence, and besides, Granny was digging her fingers into his arm so hard that he couldn't have moved even if he'd wanted to.

And where was the dog? At any minute he might start barking and then they were sure to be discovered.

The footsteps were drawing nearer and nearer. Whoever it was would be coming round the bend any second now.

Granny made a snap decision.

"Fred," she hissed urgently, "Hold the trailer steady and I'll climb in. You get on the bike and pedal like mad back towards the hotel. If anyone gets in the way, just run him over. But be quick."

Fred swallowed. His hands were shaking as he hurriedly helped Granny into the trailer and tugged the tarpaulin over her. He grabbed the handlebars and was just about to mount the bike, when, sure enough, Monty barked somewhere behind him.

The dog! He couldn't leave the dog. He turned round quickly to see if he was near enough for him to grab hold of his collar, but at that moment a very large figure came into view. It was Hamish.

Fred quickly hid behind a tree. He didn't know what to do. How could he pedal like mad along the path and knock Hamish down? It would be like smashing into the side of a mountain.

"Fergal!" Hamish called as he strode down the path. "Where are ye, you stupid man?"

"I'm here, no thanks to you," an angry voice replied, trying to heave itself out of the water. "This outfit weighs a ton when it's wet!"

As Fred watched, Hamish leant forwards, offered a giant hand to Fergal and tugged him up on to the bank.

"What do ye mean 'no thanks to me'?"

"I've told ye before, if you start showing off and swimming too fast I canna keep up with you. I'm not such a good swimmer as you. I only just passed ma Confidence. That's why the costume split in half, because you were going too fast. I thought I was a gonner- and the Monster costume is for sure."

"Ye have no idea how hard it is to lead from the front, especially when I'm dragging a dead weight like you behind me. And I couldna help it if this stupid head was coming unstuck and dangling over ma eyes. I couldna see a thing."

"Anyway," Fergal added, "you'd better stop yer moaning and get that thing off you. You're serving dinner in five minutes and yer all wet."

Hamish sighed, struggled out of the sopping Monster outfit and then shuffled over to the trailer. He lifted up the tarpaulin. Fred stopped breathing. He hardly dared look. Any minute now and Hamish would look inside the trailer and spot Granny.

"I'll go and start serving and you lock everything away. We'll hang what's left of the costume up later to dry. I'll tell the boss you're on your way, so don't be long."

He threw the heavy, wet costume into the trailer and Fred heard a loud grunt as it landed on top of Granny.

"Did ye say something?" Hamish called, setting off in a hurry down the path.

"No," Fergal replied, rummaging round in the bushes for his trainers - but Hamish had already gone.

Fred could only watch in horror as Fergal climbed onto the bike. He set off down the path, towing the trailer and Granny away, pedalling like mad, wearing his doorman's uniform and only one trainer.

# Chapter 26

Fred had no choice but to follow Fergal and the trailer. He had tried calling the dog, as loudly as he dared, but there was no reply. There was nothing else he could do. In any case, it was Granny he was worried about now.

What would happen when Fergal found her in the trailer as he was bound to do? How would she explain what she was doing there?

He stuck close to the bushes where he noticed the darkest shadows were, but, surprisingly, they hadn't gone very far when Fergal pulled up. He had stopped by the wooden shed. So he wasn't going back to the hotel then?

As Fred watched, he propped the bike up against a large oak tree and fished in his pocket for a key. This, he used to unlock the padlock that was securing a gate in the fence. He opened the gate and then struggled to manoeuvre the bike and trailer inside.

"Huh! This trailer's taking some moving today," Fergal muttered to himself. "It must be all the water in the costume that's weighing it down and making it so heavy."

This time, he propped the bike and trailer against the wooden shed and then shut, and locked, the gate behind him. Then he began running down the path in the direction of the hotel.

Fred waited until Fergal had disappeared from view, then he rushed to the fence. At least the trailer hadn't been put in the shed with the dangerous generator and all those live wires.

"Granny! Granny! Can you hear me? Are you all right?" he shouted, his voice full of panic.

"Yes and yes," came back the muffled reply. "Of course I can hear you and of course I'm all right!"

"Don't worry. I'm going to run to the hotel and tell Mr. MacNoodle where you are and he'll come and rescue you!"

"Oh no you don't, Sonny Jim!" a rough voice said, right behind him. Fred gasped in shock as his arm was seized and pulled roughly up his back. It was Fergal!

"You're hurting me!" he squealed.

"I'll do more than that to you, you interfering little busybody. I'll teach you a lesson you won't forget. And who were you talking to, eh?"

"I've lost my dog and I was looking for a lead," Fred gasped.

Just then, a volley of barks erupted from somewhere behind the hut. A few seconds later

Monty appeared carrying a battered looking trainer in his mouth.

"You were talking to your dog were you? Well that's just plain stupid. And hey! *That's* the trainer I've been searching for. Can't wait on tables with only one shoe, the boss is sure to say. I'll take that if you don't mind," he shouted, lunging at the dog. But Monty had other ideas. He took one look at Fergal and dashed off, back into the bushes. As it happened, the trainer must have been too smelly for even the dog, because he stopped when he was at a safe distance, wrinkled his nose, opened his mouth in disgust and dropped it.

Fergal unlocked the gate in the fence once more and angrily shoved Fred inside.

"You can stay there for a wee while until Hamish and I have decided what to do with you. Who knows, there might even be another Monster in the loch tonight!" he laughed. Then ferreting around in his trouser pocket he fished out a filthy, revolting looking handkerchief.

"You can't do this!" Fred shouted. "You wait 'til my dad finds out. Then you'll be sorry."

"Now I'm really scared," Fergal laughed, grabbing hold of him and tying the handkerchief tightly round his mouth. Fred kicked and struggled, but it was no good. Fergal opened the shed door, hunted around until he found a bit of string and used it to tie his hands behind his back. "That should shut you up! Now you have to admit, you've got this coming, *mate*. You've been poking your nose in where it doesn't belong ever since you got here. Oh, yes you have. *And* you moved our trailer yesterday – you can't deny it – we saw you. You upset our plans, you did. Just as well we were both free this evening, but it's been one huge rush I can tell you – and it's all your fault."

And so saying, he shut and locked the shed door and then the gate and began hunting on the ground for his trainer.

Fred's shoulder was hurting from where he had been pushed roughly against the shed wall and he felt as if he was going to be sick with the foul handkerchief stuffed in his mouth, but he forgot all about his discomfort when Granny suddenly shot out of the trailer like a jack-in-the-box. She threw the Monster costume off her, blew some pieces of weed out of her eyes and clambered up on to the saddle of the bike.

"Mind out of the way Fred," she commanded as she selected an arrow from her handbag, pulled back the string of her bow and aimed it at Fergal.

"Mmmmm, ug, ug ug ug!" Fred spluttered. She was going to kill him!

But Granny was far too busy squinting along the arrow, lining it up with her target to bother with Fred. Five out of ten hits was a record that was just there to be broken.

As Fergal was straightening up, having returned his foot to his scruffy trainer (as unlike Cinderella trying the glass slipper as it's possible to imagine) a satisfying 'whooshing' sound could be heard as Granny's arrow sliced through the air.

'Thwack! It ripped through the sleeve of his doorman's uniform and embedded itself in the tree.

"Aaaah!" Fergal screamed.

The arrow hadn't actually clipped him; it was the shock of it that made him yell. One minute he was mobile, the next he was stuck fast, all movement temporarily suspended.

"Who did that?" he yelled crossly. "Whoever it was I'll make you sorry!"

Granny punched the air and the bike wobbled dangerously. Then she climbed down carefully, wincing a bit because of her arthritis as she did so, and turned triumphantly to Fred. She untied his hands and the pongy handkerchief.

"Yuck!" Fred spat, scrubbing at his mouth with the back of his hand. Then, "Nice shot!" he exclaimed proudly.

"Well, not really," Granny said modestly. "I was aiming for his leg."

"Here!" Fergal called as he tried, without success, to tug himself away from the tree. "Pull this arrow out will you? I'm supposed to be serving dinner right now. Hamish'll be hopping mad with me as it is - and so will the boss."

"You should have thought of that before you started threatening my grandson. Besides, you've locked us in here so we can't get out, in case you'd forgotten," Granny said crossly.

"I didn't mean to," Fergal whimpered. "I didn't even know you were in there, honest, old lady. And I'm a *doorman* not a villain. I hold doors open for people like you and carry their cases and everything. And serve dinner sometimes," he added.

But no one was listening to him.

"What are we going to do next?" Fred said, pulling bits of weed and leaves from Granny's hair. "Are you going to phone my dad – or the police - on your mobile?"

"No, I'm not dear. First we're going to have a good look inside this shed - and then we've got the other outlaw to catch. This business has to stop." She looked at Fred's worried face. "And *then* we'll phone your dad, I promise."

# Chapter 27

Granny had been wrong, as it turned out. There was no sign of a generator at all  - or any live wires, or anything remotely dangerous looking, unless you counted a bag of tools, some pieces of balsa wood and a few sacks.

She had used her hat pin to pick the lock of the shed.

"Wow!" Fred whistled in admiration. "I didn't know you could do that. That was spectacular!"

"I thought I'd better learn after that time I locked myself out of the maisonette and you got stuck in the cat flap. Do you remember?"

Remember? He still had the scars to prove it. *And* he remembered the telling off his dad had got from the firemen for trying to tell them how to do their job.

"*Push his bottom with your foot. Flatten his ears against the sides of his head...*"

"Why don't you just unpick the lock in the fence and let us out?" he asked.

"Because I've told you, I want to have a look round and then I want to catch the other culprit. And mind where you put your feet. The wood is all rotten. I don't want any accidents. Hum!" she said mysteriously. "That gives me an idea. Pass me a claw hammer from that tool bag."

Picking his way carefully across the floor, Fred did as he was asked. At once Granny set to, wrenching up the floorboards, one after another, until she had made a large hole. "Now I need your torch," she said, holding out her hand.

Fred delved into his carry case and produced it with a flourish. He wound the handle a few times for luck.

"Hurry up and stop messing about," Granny snapped, showing a total lack of understanding of the mechanics of the thing.

Fred shrugged, switched the torch on and passed it to her. She shone it down through the hole she'd made and gave a grunt of approval. "That should do the trick."

Fred smiled as he realised what she was up to.

"A bear trap! Did you learn that at Brownies too?"

"No – at Saturday Morning Pictures back in nineteen hundred and frozen-to-death. Some baddies were trying to catch Tarzan. Now let's have a look in those sacks."

It was very dusty in the shed and there wasn't much light to see by, so they were glad of the torch.

128

Fred shone it into one of the sacks and pulled out a large monster's head made out of sacking. It had been very badly sewn together with red wool and had rough, jagged slits for eyes.

"So this is where they stash all their stuff. The danger signs were put there to warn people away and stop them from snooping."

"I don't think this would fool anybody do you?" Fred said, putting the head on and sneezing half a dozen times as the dust drifted up his nostrils.

"We'll soon find out," Granny replied. "Leave it on – it suits you. What else is in there?"

They searched through the other sacks and found rubber inflatable monsters and various body parts made out of assorted scraps of material. Fred examined some of them.

"Look there's a large hole in this. I bet this is the outfit my bit of cloth came from."

"Come on Fred. Put that on as well and then go and sit over by that wall. If my guess is right, we won't have long to wait. I'll just camouflage this hole and open the door..." she said. "And then we'll wait."

# Chapter 28

This time Granny was right! There wasn't long to wait. Fred was timing it on his watch. A problem sprang into his head:

If it takes *two* men *one* hour to serve dinner, how long would it take *one* man?

He was worried. His mum and dad were sure to be back from Inverness by now and they would be going frantic. He was also concerned for the dog. He could be anywhere. It was a pity, Fred thought, that he wasn't like Lassie. *She* would have travelled miles, through mine fields if necessary, to lead his parents to him. Monty was way too dim and weedy for that.

It was dark in the shed. He couldn't see Granny unless he shone his torch on her, and even then he could just make out a shadowy lump. She looked just like another sack hiding behind the door and he was sure he could hear her snoring.

She sat up, though, the minute she heard raised voices outside. They both did.

"What do you think you're messing about at Fergal?" Hamish was saying in a very loud voice. "I had to serve that lot their haggis and chips all by myself."

"I couldna help it. I didna do it on purpose. I'm stuck."

"What do you mean you're stuck? Come away from that tree and explain yerself."

"I 'm trying to tell you I *can't*. I've been bolted to it."

Hamish stamped over to him to take a closer look.

"It's an arrow," he said, scratching his head. "How did that get there?"

"That little old lady, the one who keeps coming to the hotel looking for freebies! She shot me with her bow," Fergal whimpered.

"Come off it! Do you take me for a fool?" Hamish snorted.

Fergal was about to reply, when he thought better of it.

"She's in there," he said instead, trying to point with his free hand.

Hamish turned to look and that was when he noticed that the shed door was standing wide open.

"What did you leave the door open for, you idiot? Anybody could see what's in there."

"I didn't leave it open. She must've opened it."

Hamish walked to the fence to investigate.

"'Ere, don't leave me stuck to this tree mate," Fergal pleaded. "Get me off it."

"Take your jacket off! The arrow went through your jacket, not your brain."

"But it went through my shirt as well."

"Then take your shirt off," Hamish called over his shoulder, feeling pretty exasperated.

He was still muttering to himself as he unlocked the gate in the fence and walked up to the shed. He clenched his fists and ground his teeth together.

"Just you wait 'til I get my hands on you," he muttered. "Interfering ..."

He knocked on the door, even though it was already open.

"Hello! Are you in there little old lady?" he called in an oh-so-gentle tone.

"Yes I am dear," Granny replied, in her sweetest, kindest voice. "Come on in. I've got something for you."

Hamish shaped his hands into fists, stepped over the threshold onto the piece of sacking, and down he crashed through the hole in the floorboards, into the pit below.

Granny clapped her hands with delight.

"One down and one more to go!" she whispered.

Next came Fergal, but he was rather more timid. He stood by the doorway, wearing a grubby white shirt with one of the sleeves hanging off, calling nervously,

"Hamish are you in there mate?"

When there was no reply, he inched his way forwards, into the room. He hovered with his feet *very* close to the piece of sacking.

From her station behind the door, Granny was willing him to take just one more step.

This was the moment that Fred, still wearing a monster's head, suddenly made a very loud roaring noise. At the same time, he switched on his torch and held it under his chin so that the blue beam shone through the eyes and cast grotesque shadows on the shed walls.

"Aaaaargh!" Fergal screamed.

After that, it took Granny just one gentle push and down he went to join Hamish a few metres below. As Fergal landed with a thud on top of him, Hamish immediately tried to force his huge head back up through the hole in the floorboards, but Granny pushed him back with her size sevens.

"Now can we go and get help?" Fred said.

But as it happened, they didn't need to. The noises they could hear outside, and the all the lights they could see flashing, soon told them that help had come to them. Fred set off his alarm clock just in case the rescue team couldn't hear them shouting and see his torch waving about.

"Fred Boggitt where have you been?" Mrs. Boggitt yelled, the minute Fred set foot outside. "You naughty, naughty boy, worrying your mother like that," she scolded, hugging him and smothering him with kisses.

"Fred, I'm feeling very cross. I bought some chump chops at the butcher's in Inverness and they've been cooking for over two hours. They'll be burned to a cinder," Mr. Boggitt said. "And I don't think you've been looking after your Granny properly either, have you? She's got bits of weed sticking out of her hair. Have you been swimming in the loch Granny? Ha! Ha!"

"Did Monty come and find you?" Fred asked him optimistically, seeing the dog, on its lead, sitting nicely. Perhaps he was more intelligent and obedient than Fred gave him credit for.

"He did not. But I do believe that he went to find Mr. MacNoodle and *he* came to find us. And it's a good job he did as it turns out. Now will someone please tell me what's going on?"

"Well now, ladies and gentlemen, may I suggest that we go back to your hotel, Mr. MacNoodle, and continue this conversation in comfort," one of the policemen said. "I think this wee laddie has had enough excitement for one day – and his Granny too."

Just at that moment there was the sound of a scuffle and some angry shouting coming from the shed, as a group of policemen escorted Hamish and Fergal down the path.

As they drew level with Mr. MacNoodle, Hamish turned. "I'm sorry, dad," he said. "We did it for you."

Fred and Granny gasped in surprise.

"*Hamish is your son?*" they said in unison.

"They, um, both are," Mr. MacNoodle said sadly. "I know it doesn't look like it, but they're twins.

Fergal takes after me and Hamish looks like his mother."

"Will someone please tell me what's going on?" Mr. Boggitt shouted again, looking as if he might explode at any minute.

# Chapter 29

It was half an hour later and Fred and Granny had done their best to explain everything that had happened, despite several interruptions from Mr. and Mrs. Boggitt.

"You should have told me what you were doing, Fred. A parent has the right to know," Mr. Boggitt said.

"But you said I wasn't to talk about..."

"Don't answer your father back Poppet," Mrs. Boggitt added.

"You *said* you were going on a boat trip!"

"We *did* go on a ..."

"Fred, I told you not to..."

"I think we'll just talk to them both quietly," Sergeant Macduff suggested. "Is there some place that we could talk to the three of you in private, Mr. MacNoodle?"

After that, Mr. and Mrs. Boggitt found themselves being escorted into the lounge, where the residents were busy watching a football match. A policeman had already had a quick word with the guests, giving them a brief outline of what had been happening.

Mr. MacNoodle invited everyone else into his private study, where Fred and Granny explained, in some detail, their version of events.

"You've been very foolish wee laddie – and you Granny. You could have been badly hurt, going off like that on your own, investigating matters that are no concern of yours. You've been *very foolish indeed.* That's our job, that is."

Sergeant Macduff had seated himself on a black leather swivel chair, underneath a painting of a fierce-looking Scotsman wearing a lot of tartan and a huge red beard.

"Do you know, the man in that picture puts me in mind of Braveheart MacBoggitt. Do you suppose we could be related, Mr. MacNoodle?"

"Um, no!" Mr. MacNoodle said quickly, blushing to the roots of his hair. "I only know him as Big Mac. I never found out his surname unfortunately, but I know he did something really shameful and wicked. Och, no, ye wouldna want to be related to *him* I can tell ye."

Granny glanced at Fred and slipped down in her leather chair. It squeaked loudly as she did so.

"As I was saying..." Sergeant Macduff continued hastily, "you could have been hurt..."

"Oh my boys would never have hurt them," Mr. MacNoodle interrupted quickly. "They're good boys really, only I've found it a bit hard trying to bring them up on ma own, ever since their mother took off with a sword-swallower from Edinburgh. And what with trying to run the hotel and everything..."

"I'm going to take your word that you knew nothing about what they were up to. I've known you long enough to trust you on that. And you did do the right thing in contacting the Boggitts, and us, when the dog appeared with the wee laddie's binoculars and trapped Hamish in the broom cupboard until he confessed to you what Fergal had done to him. *But* - it's not the first time they've been in trouble is it, Dougal?" Sergeant Macduff persisted, swivelling in his seat and finding himself facing the wrong way. "Ahem! There was the time they were trying to pass off bits of coal as fossilized Monster droppings..."

"But they were only trying to help me. Money was a bit short...."

"And that time they were selling photos of the Loch Ness Monster doing back stroke? Now we can't have members of the public being fooled this way. No wonder no one ever believes we even *have* a Monster in these parts – well only the visitors who are stupi... Ahem!"

Not long after this, Sergeant Macduff took his leave and Mr. MacNoodle followed Granny and Fred into the lounge.

This time the residents had their backs to the loch. The chairs had been turned towards the television so that they could enjoy the big match.

Mrs. Boggitt, who was not interested in football in the slightest, had dropped a stitch in her knitting and had a lot of unpicking to do. Mr. Boggitt was standing behind Morag's chair, refereeing the match.

"*Pass the ball!* No, not to him, to someone on your own side!" he shouted at the screen. "G-O-A-L! *I don't believe it. He's missed it. An open goal and he's missed it!*" he screamed, banging his fist up and down on the back of Morag's chair.

"That number 7 is playing like a girl," he called in disgust.

"That number 7 just happens to be our son," Mr. Campbell remarked.

"And which side are you meant to be supporting?" Morag asked sarcastically, swivelling her head round to look at him.

"I dunno," Mr. Boggitt replied. "Who's playing?"

No one seemed to have noticed Fred, Granny and Mr. MacNoodle slip into the room, apart from Brenda that is, who took one look at them, muttered something about 'having a harmless bit of fun totally ruined', and then turned her eyes back to the screen.

Fred was feeling rather let down, after all the excitement of the past few hours. Like his mum, he wasn't interested in football. He stood next to Granny, looking out at the loch.

It was really dark outside by this time and he could see the lights of the hotel, and the television, reflected in the window. But, cupping his eyes against the glass and peering through it, he noticed that the water was fairly still and looked inky black.

As he watched quietly, a million thoughts spinning through his head, the moon, as big as a football, spun out from behind a cloud. It hung over the loch, sending out a huge, powerful, silver spotlight. Fred shivered and turned to look at Granny. As he did so, out of the corner of his eye he noticed a huge, dark, majestic shape swimming effortlessly into the circle of light.

"Dad!" he croaked. "Dad! Everybody!"

"Penalty!" Mr. Boggitt screamed behind him.

"Where's your glasses, man? That was no penalty," Mr. Campbell shouted back.

But Granny had seen what Fred had seen. Beside him, she stood as still as one of the portraits that hung on the wall, staring in admiration.

The Loch Ness Monster passed in front of the hotel, heading towards the weeds, but before it reached them it seemed to change its mind. Instead, it turned and sailed back through the light, then carried on swimming, heading up the loch and leaving behind it a wide, silvery wake. Fred smiled. So it *did* have four humps after all!

"Ahem, excuse me," a voice said behind them, making them jump. It was Mr. MacNoodle.

"Did you see it?" Fred spluttered, so excited that he could hardly speak.

"See what laddie? Oh, the game you mean? Och no, I'm more of a tossing the caber sort of person myself. No, I've come to ask if you and your family would care to join me for dinner, in my private dining room. I don't believe you've eaten yet."

Fred thought about his father's burnt chops.

"Yeah!" he said. "That would be spectacular. Thank you."

# Chapter 30

"**W**ell you've certainly got wonderful chefs here, I must say," Mr. Boggitt said happily, a little while later, sitting back in his chair. "Remind me to ask them for some of their recipes. And, um, I hope this spot of bother won't mean that people stop coming to your hotel. I mean, it seems quite a nice place."

"I hope so too. Anyway, we're fully booked for the foreseeable future and my regulars say they'll be back as usual. Some of them still think they've seen the real Monster you know in spite of everything they've been told. Never mind, we live in hope, Mr. Boggitt. And what will you be doing for the rest of the week?" Mr. MacNoodle asked.

"I hope you'll still be coming to see us for your – er – refreshments," he said, looking at Fred and Granny.

But Mr. Boggitt spoke before anyone else had the chance to reply.

"Auntie Ethel phoned to say that she's managed to hire someone to help her until Enid is fit for work. So, Fred, you and I will hire a couple of bikes. We'll head into the woods, away from all the tourists. We'll light a fire; do a spot of fishing; throw a couple of salmon on the barbie. You know. Oh… and if anyone wants to come with us, of course…?"

"No, Fred senior," Mrs. Boggitt said emphatically.

"No," Granny said. "I'll get my laughs sitting outside my tent with my feet up, thank you very much."